THE SPECTRE FROM THE MAGICIAN'S MUSEUM

Also by John Bellairs

THE SPECTRE FROM THE MAGICIAN'S MUSEUM

JOHN BELLAIRS

By BRAD STRICKLAND

Piccadilly

PRESS

First published in Great Britain in 2020 by
Piccadilly Press
80-81 Wimpole St, London W1G 9RE
www.piccadillypress.co.uk

First published in the United States of America
by Dial Books for Young Readers, 1998

A CIP catalogue record for this book is available
from the British Library.

ISBN: 978-1-84812-822-4
Also available as an ebook

1 3 5 7 9 10 8 6 4 2

Typeset in Sabon LT Std by Palimpsest Book Production Ltd,
Falkirk, Stirlingshire

Printed and bound by Clays Ltd, Elcograf S.p.A.

Piccadilly Press is an imprint of Bonnier Books UK
www.bonnierbooks.co.uk

For Bob and Elaine Lund,
whose museum shows that the secret
of magic is people.
B.S.

CHAPTER ONE

Lewis Barnavelt had been frightened before in his life, but this time he was terrified.

It was a sunny, warm autumn day. Lewis stood just outside the junior high school in the small town of New Zebedee, and felt his stomach fluttering with a million butterflies. "What am I going to *do*?" he muttered.

Lewis was a chunky boy of about thirteen. He had a round, anxious face and a timid way of looking at the world. Now he was waiting for his friend, Rose Rita Pottinger. They were both in the same grade and in the same situation, and Lewis hoped that talking to her would make him feel better.

Lewis stood with his back against the wall, and when Dave Shellenberger and Tom Lutz came running out of the school, he pressed against the black stones as if he wanted to sink into them and disappear. Dave and Tom had been big wheels all through elementary school, and now they were two of the most popular kids in junior high. Both were great at sports, good-looking, and snazzy dressers. By contrast Lewis was clumsy and heavy. Instead of nylon shirts and jeans, he wore flannel shirts and corduroy trousers that went *whip-whip* when he walked. He was not popular either. Sometimes he thought the only people in the world who liked him were his uncle Jonathan Barnavelt, their next-door neighbour Mrs Zimmermann, and his English pen pal, Bertie Goodring. Plus Rose Rita, of course.

At last Lewis saw her coming out of the school. Rose Rita was sort of like Lewis—

another odd duck. She was tall for her age, and skinny, with long, straight, black hair and big, round, black-rimmed glasses. Lewis knew that Rose Rita regarded herself as an ugly duckling. People thought she was a tomboy too, and she hated the blouses and plaid skirts her mum insisted she wear to school. She felt much more comfortable in sweatshirts, jeans, and trainers. Rose Rita paused outside the school door, clutching her books to her chest. Then she saw Lewis and gave him a dismal smile. As she came down the steps, she muttered, "It's awful."

Lewis nodded glumly. "What are we going to do?"

Rose Rita rolled her eyes. "I know what I'd *like* to do. I'd like to sail away on a slow boat to China. Or get sick with a disease that would last exactly four weeks!"

"Sure," said Lewis sarcastically. "Or run off and join the circus, or find a formula to make you the Invisible Girl. Only we can't do any of those things." The two trudged away from the school, heading for Rose Rita's house. Normally

Lewis liked to walk down the streets of New Zebedee, at least when no bullies like Woody Mingo were around. New Zebedee was a small town. Its downtown stretched only three blocks long, but the buildings all looked as if they had stories hidden inside them. The old brick shops had high false fronts, and the houses were elaborate Victorian structures with towers, cupolas, and wide, rambling porches. At the west end of Main Street stood a wonderful fountain that spumed a crystal willow tree of water from inside a circle of marble columns. At the east end were the G.A.R. Hall and the Civil War Monument and East End Park. In between were dozens of places that promised excitement and plenty to do.

Except today none of it appealed to Lewis. Because in just four weeks he had to face—

Lewis swallowed. "I don't want to be in any stupid talent show," he complained.

"I'm not thrilled about it myself," snapped Rose Rita. They walked in silence past Heemsoth's Rexall Drug Store, its windows still full of back-to-school items. Lewis and Rose Rita turned off Main Street and plodded up Mansion Street, past the Masonic temple. Rose Rita lived with her dad and mum at 39 Mansion Street, and Lewis waited in the living room while she changed out of her school clothes. After a few minutes she came out again, wearing a ratty old Notre Dame sweatshirt, jeans, and black trainers. The two of them walked towards High Street in a miserable silence.

Lewis lived at 100 High Street with his uncle Jonathan. Both of Lewis's parents had died in a terrible car accident when Lewis was younger. He had moved to New Zebedee soon afterwards, and now Uncle Jonathan was his legal guardian. Jonathan Barnavelt was a friendly man with red hair, a bushy red beard streaked here and there with white, and a potbelly. He smiled a lot, laughed easily and loudly, and was rich because he had inherited a lot of money from his grandfather.

Even better, Jonathan Barnavelt was a sorcerer. He could create wonderful illusions, not by trickery, but by real, honest-to-goodness magic. The previous June, to celebrate the end of school, Jonathan had re-created the Battle of Lepanto, the great naval fight between the Christians and the Turks in 1571. The battle had proved a terrific sight, as galleys clashed and a thousand cannons roared. It had delighted both Lewis and Rose Rita, who knew the names of all the different kinds of cannons, from carronades to long nines. In fact, Rose Rita had pointed out that the carronades really didn't belong, because they had not been invented until the eighteenth century.

Remembering the excitement, Lewis grumbled, "Too bad Uncle Jonathan can't help us."

"Maybe he will," said a thoughtful Rose Rita.

Lewis shook his head. "He says I have to do what the school tells me. It's not fair using magic. That's the same as cheating."

"Even in an emergency?" asked Rose Rita. "This is practically a matter of life and death."

They were trudging up the hill towards the summit and Lewis's house. "I should have known this would happen," groaned Lewis. "Every year the elementary-school kids get to see the junior-high talent show. I just never thought about how they got all those junior-high kids to go onstage and make fools of themselves."

"Now you know," said Rose Rita. "They force them." They reached Lewis's house, a tall old mansion with a tower in front. Fastened to a black wrought-iron fence was the number 100 in red reflecting numerals. Lewis and Rose Rita passed through the gate, across the yard, and up the steps, both still steeped in gloom.

They found Lewis's uncle in the parlour, fiddling with something he had recently bought for the house—a Zenith Stratosphere television. The boxy walnut cabinet looked pretty snazzy. When you opened the front doors of the cabinet, you revealed the television screen, a radio, and a phonograph. The TV screen was perfectly circular, like a porthole. With the spidery antenna that Uncle Jonathan had attached to one of the chimneys, the TV could pick up three channels. The pictures were black and white and so filled with static and snow that sometimes it was hard to tell if you were watching a western adventure or a quiz show.

Uncle Jonathan looked up cheerfully as Lewis and Rose Rita came in. "Hi," he said, thumping the top of the set. As usual, he was wearing tan work trousers, a blue shirt, and his red vest. He stepped back from the TV, stuck his thumbs in the bottom pockets of his vest, tilted his head to one side, and asked, "How's that?"

Rose Rita squinted at the dim picture. "It's hard to say. What's it supposed to be?"

With a snort, Jonathan replied, "That's just the trouble—I can't tell!"

"Then it doesn't matter," said Rose Rita promptly.

Uncle Jonathan threw his head back and laughed. "Good point, Rose Rita!" He switched off the TV, and the picture shrank to a tiny white dot in the centre of the blank screen before disappearing.

Lewis asked, "May we have a snack, Uncle Jonathan?"

His uncle pulled out his pocket watch. "Hmm. I suppose so. Just one glass of milk and a couple of cookies each. Florence has promised to make dinner for us tonight, and I don't want her thinking we don't appreciate her cooking."

"Great," said Lewis, perking up. Florence Zimmermann, their next-door neighbour, was a fantastic cook. She also happened to be a witch. Not an evil witch, but a friendly, twinkly-eyed, wrinkly-faced good witch whose magical abilities were even greater than Uncle Jonathan's. "Can Rose Rita have dinner with us?"

"Sure," said Uncle Jonathan. "Just call your parents and get permission, Rose Rita. Frizzy Wig and I will cook an extra portion."

Rose Rita called, and her mother cheerfully said Rose Rita could stay. Later that afternoon Rose Rita and Lewis lay on their stomachs in the parlour, watching the TV and wondering what they could possibly do for the school talent show. Uncle Jonathan and Mrs

Zimmermann were bustling around in the kitchen, rattling pots and pans and producing wonderful aromas. Lewis wasn't really paying much attention to the TV. He and Rose Rita were watching a kids' show, with ancient black-and-white cartoons. Cats chased mice, and pigs sang, and kangaroos boxed. All the animals were drawn as collections of circles, and it was hard to tell the cartoon pigs from cartoon elks or spiny echidnas.

"Maybe you could dance," said Lewis. "You like to dance."

"Huh!" snorted Rose Rita. "There's a big difference between dancing with other people and dancing alone onstage. No thanks."

Lewis sighed and fell silent. The cartoon ended. A clown, dressed in a baggy white outfit, his face covered with white makeup, appeared on the screen. His nose might have been round and red, but it looked like a black bubble on the black-and-white TV. He had painted-on, high, arched eyebrows and a wide smiling mouth. He wore a ruffled collar and a funny hat, shaped like a milk bottle complete with a flat paper lid. "Kids!" said the announcer, who always sounded as if he were on the verge of a heart attack. "Here's your friend and mine, the amazing Creamy the Magical Clown!"

"Thank you," Creamy said in a nimbly voice. The camera pulled back to show that Creamy was standing beside a little girl about seven or eight years old. "I have a helper today!"

Rose Rita said, "She looks scared to death."

Creamy held a microphone down to the little girl and asked her name.

"Edith Arabella Elizabeth Bonny McPeters," she said shyly.

"My goodness!" exclaimed Creamy. "Your parents just didn't know when to stop, did they?"

Edith shook her head and smiled. Lewis saw that she was missing two front teeth.

"Well, Edith Arabella Elizabeth Bonny," said Creamy, "do you like flowers?"

The little girl nodded.

"Good!" said Creamy. Someone handed him a

sheet of newspaper. He held it up and turned it so the camera could see both sides. Music began to play. Creamy shook out the sheet of paper, rolled it up, shaped it into a cone, and gave it to Edith. "Hold this," instructed the clown. The music paused. Creamy turned to the camera. "Now boys and girls, say the magic words!"

The kids in the studio audience all bellowed out, "Twin Oaks milk is the milk for me!"

"Oh!" said Edith, blinking. A bouquet of daisies had sprung up out of the cone of newspapers. The band played a hearty *Tah-dah*!

"You keep those pretty flowers," Creamy rumbled, laughing. The little girl nodded and clutched the bouquet to her chest. Creamy patted her on the head and then looked at the camera. "And now let's hear from our good friends at Twin Oaks Dairy!"

Lewis sprang up and switched off the set. "That's it!" he said with a triumphant grin. "That's the answer to our problem!"

"Twin Oaks milk?" asked Rose Rita, raising her eyebrows. "I don't get it."

"Not milk—magic," replied Lewis. He swept his arms wide and bowed to an imaginary audience. "We'll do a magic act!"

Rose Rita shook her head. "Your uncle would never let you get away with it."

"Not real magic," said Lewis impatiently. "Stage magic, like Creamy the Clown does. Tricks with ropes and rings and stuff. What do you call it—conjuring! I can be the magician, and you can be my beautiful assistant!"

"Hmm." Rose Rita sat up and adjusted her glasses. Her expression became grudgingly thoughtful. "I don't know—maybe. Do you know any magic tricks?"

Lewis sat again, collapsing to the floor like a punctured balloon. "No," he admitted. "Not really."

"We can ask your uncle," suggested Rose Rita. "He entertains at the PTA, and everyone thinks his tricks are just conjuring."

"Maybe some of them are," said Lewis, thinking it over. "I've never really asked him."

Just then Jonathan Barnavelt called from the

dining room in a booming voice: "Kids! Dinner's ready! Come and get it, or I'll throw it to the hogs!"

"You will do no such thing, Brush Mush!" said the outraged voice of Mrs Zimmermann. "Not after I worked so hard over this hot stove, you won't!"

"Come on," said Lewis with a grin, and he and Rose Rita raced to the dining room.

CHAPTER TWO

Even though Lewis knew all about Mrs Zimmermann's culinary talents, this time he had to admit she had outdone herself. Dinner was a succulent, perfectly browned roast, so tender that it practically melted in Lewis's mouth, together with luscious, buttery whipped potatoes that were just right, not too dry and not too gloopy. Uncle Jonathan used a ladle to make a little well in the top of each mound of mashed potatoes, and he poured in some rich brown gravy. Mrs Zimmermann had also cooked candied carrots and petite green peas with baby pearl onions, and there was a big apple pie for dessert. "This feast is in honour of school starting again," Mrs Zimmermann explained, a pleased twinkle in her eye as she saw how much Lewis and Rose Rita liked the food. "I know how this can be a hard time in life, and I thought a celebration might be in order."

"It's wonderful, Pruny Face," said Jonathan Barnavelt with a chuckle. He patted his stomach. "Still, we'll have to watch it for the rest of the week. I've put on weight since I gave up smoking!"

"Then feast today and fast tomorrow," replied Mrs Zimmermann tartly. She was a trim, elderly woman with an untidy nest of white hair, and she was wearing a purple floral dress. Florence Zimmermann loved the colour purple, and her house was full of purple furnishings, rugs, wallpaper and even the toilet paper. "More carrots, Rose Rita?" she asked.

For a little while Lewis gave all his attention

to the wonderful meal. Finally, as he watched his uncle bring in the golden-brown apple pie, Lewis felt Rose Rita kick him under the table. He looked at her in surprise. "Ask him," Rose Rita mouthed.

Lewis cleared his throat. "Uh, Uncle Jonathan," he said, "do you know anything about stage magic? Conjuring?"

Uncle Jonathan raised his red eyebrows as he put a slice of pie on a small plate and passed it to Rose Rita. "Oh, a little," he said. "I can do some nifty card tricks that don't depend on real magic. Why do you ask?"

Lewis explained the problem he and Rose Rita faced. Mrs Zimmermann shook her head and sighed. "That's one thing I never liked to do when I was teaching school—force a student to get up onstage and perform in front of others," she said. "Oh, I know it's supposed to give you poise and confidence, but it always seemed cruel to me. Not everyone has the kind of talents that shine out from a stage. Some of us are more quiet and private."

"Hmm," said Uncle Jonathan. "I agree with Florence, but it seems to me that we still have a problem. The talent show is an old tradition, and you know how teachers hate to disturb tradition. So your idea is to do a magic show, is it?"

"Yes, but just conjuring tricks, not real magic," Lewis said quickly.

"Good," his uncle replied. "Real magic can get you into a world of trouble—as you know very well. Florence, I think Lewis and Rose Rita ought to consult Mr Robert Hardwick. What do you say?"

Mrs Zimmermann's bright blue eyes shone. "That's a wonderful idea, Weird Beard! If anyone in town could help them put an act together, Bob Hardwick is the man!"

"Who's he?" asked Rose Rita. "I never heard of him."

Uncle Jonathan passed a slice of pie to Lewis and laughed. "Bob Hardwick is a retired newspaperman and an amateur conjuror. He can do some amazing tricks with ropes and steel rings. He used to do shows for schools—called himself Marcus the Great. Well, he retired a few months ago and moved from Detroit to New Zebedee. He has a huge collection of magical memorabilia—things like original Houdini posters and a little cannon that the great Blackstone once used in his act—and he's putting these items into a museum that he plans to open downtown in the old Eugster Brewery building."

Mrs Zimmermann winked. "Mr Hardwick thinks your uncle is a conjuror too," she confided. "When you see him, please keep the Capharnaum County Magicians Society a secret. Mr Hardwick doesn't know there are real sorcerers and witches about."

Lewis nodded. He always kept his uncle's magical hobby to himself. Once, years before, he had asked Uncle Jonathan to show off to impress a friend of his named Tarby Corrigan. Unfortunately, Uncle Jonathan's magical eclipse of the moon had frightened Tarby. Lewis had lost a friend. Except for the other members of the Capharnaum County Magicians Society, now only Rose Rita knew about the real magic that Uncle Jonathan and Mrs Zimmermann could command. Luckily, Rose Rita liked both of them. She knew better than to talk about their magic.

"Tell you what," Uncle Jonathan said as he served Mrs Zimmermann's pie. "I'll give Bob a call. Tomorrow's Saturday, so he'll probably be downtown. Maybe we can arrange for you to see what his museum's going to be like. And I'm sure he can help you put together some conjuring tricks."

And so it was all arranged. Early the next morning Lewis and Rose Rita went down to Main Street. The former brewery was a brick building that Lewis liked a lot. The redbrick walls were mossy and battered, and chiselled in the cornerstone was the date 1842 in swirly numerals. One side of the wall had round windows, like the tops of beer barrels, each one divided into four wedge-shaped panes. Eugster's Brewery had gone out of business years before.

As long as Lewis could remember, the building had been vacant, its front windows papered over from inside, a chain and padlock on its front door.

On Saturday morning, though, the change was obvious. The windows sparkled in the morning light, framed by maroon curtains edged in gold lace. An oblong cardboard sign, inside the window on the right, showed an old-fashioned steel engraving of a top-hatted magician levitating a woman, who lay as stiff as a board in mid-air. Above the artwork, in ornate circus-poster lettering, were the grand words:

THE NATIONAL MUSEUM OF MAGIC

Under the artwork were more words, in a smaller type. Lewis giggled as he read what they had to say:

ABSOLUTELY the finest collection of memorabilia relating to conjuring, prestidigitation, hocus-pocus, flummery, thimblerigging, sleight of hand, jiggery-pokery, and good-natured foolery known to MAN or BEAST! GUARANTEED thrills, chills, brainteasers, crowd pleasers, mind-bogglers and hornswogglers! YOU will be AMAZED!

ENDORSED by the Pulpit, the Press, and the Lectern as WHOLESOME FAMILY ENTERTAINMENT! If you are OVERCOME by the SHEER GRANDEUR of the show, the Management will provide FREE SMELLING SALTS to bring you back to FULL CONSCIOUSNESS! Come one! Come all!

—Robert W. Hardwick, Prop.

"Whoosh!" commented Rose Rita as she read the placard. "Mr Hardwick promises a lot, doesn't he?"

Lewis felt a quiver of anticipation. "I hope he can suggest something for us." He tried the door, and it swung open, jingling a bell overhead. "Hello?"

Lewis and Rose Rita looked into a long, narrow room, cluttered with all sorts of weird objects: mummy cases, steamer trunks with swords thrust into them, a huge galvanised-steel milk canister with its lid padlocked shut, shelves full of top hats, canes, wands, and handcuffs, and on every wall poster after poster advertising magicians and their shows. It was hard to see anything beyond a few feet from the door, because the lights were out. Rose Rita said, "Looks like nobody's home."

Next to the door stood an upright mummy case, six and a half feet tall. The carved and painted face at the top was cruel, with frowning eyebrows, a hooked nose, a vicious mouth, and a strange squared-off goatee. But what caught Lewis's attention were the eyes—the wooden eyelids were opening slowly, and the glaring, dead eyes stared straight at him! He could only squeak and tug at Rose Rita's arm, pointing at the thing.

"What is it—Oh!" Rose Rita stiffened as she noticed the mummy case too. Now the lips were moving.

In a grotesque, creaking voice, the mummy

case demanded, "Who dares disturb my three-thousand-year slumber? *Who?*"

Lewis gasped.

After a moment the mummy case sighed. "You're supposed to say your names, and then I can tell you to go right upstairs. This is a trick, kids. It's electric motors and a microphone and speaker. I take it you're Lewis and Rose Rita?"

Rose Rita recovered first. "Yes, we are."

"Then come on up." The mummy case's eyelids clicked shut. Then they flicked open again. "The light switch is beside the door on your left. Please close the door before you come upstairs. We're not officially open yet." The eyes clacked closed.

Lewis turned on the lights, and Rose Rita closed the door, its lock clacking loudly. Now they could see the stairway on their right. They climbed up. At the top they saw four men sitting at a table. They had been playing cards, and they all smiled as the kids walked towards them. One man, slim and about sixty, with curly grey hair and glasses, stood. "I'm sorry I startled you," he said, holding up a silvery microphone shaped like a flattened baseball. "I couldn't resist." He put the microphone down and shook hands with Lewis. "Mr Lewis Barnavelt, I presume?"

"Yes," Lewis answered. "And this is Rose Rita Pottinger."

"Charmed to meet you," replied the man. "I am Robert Hardwick, and with my dear wife, Ellen, I own this establishment. You can call me Bob, if you like. These are my Saturday poker buddies. Allow me to introduce Mr Clarence Mussenberger, Mr Thomas Perkins, and Mr Johnny Stone."

Each of the men stood to shake hands. Mr Mussenberger was stocky and round faced, with cheerful brown eyes. He looked familiar, somehow. Mr Perkins was very tall and thin, with distinguished streaks of grey in his black hair. And Mr Stone was unusually short—even shorter than Lewis—with a mischievous glint in his eye and a double chin. He was almost completely bald, except for a fringe of grey hair.

"Well now," Mr Hardwick said, bringing over a couple of folding chairs for Lewis and Rose Rita. "Your uncle Jonathan says you need help. Tell him that one of these days I'm going to figure out how he does that trick with the three candles and the ace of spades! But now, what do you need?"

Feeling embarrassed, Lewis stammered out his problem. "So Rose Rita and I thought we might put together a magic act," he finished.

Mr Mussenberger cleared his throat. "You need about five good, quick tricks," he rumbled.

Rose Rita blinked. "Oh, my gosh! You're Creamy the Magical Clown, from TV!"

The men all laughed, but Mr Mussenberger beamed. "Pipe down, you mutts," he said to the others. "My dear, you are correct. Five days a week I am Creamy the Magical Clown, in the service of the Twin Oaks Dairy Company. On weekends, however, I am simply Clare." He nodded to the other men. "Of course, these gentlemen aren't nearly as famous as Creamy, but let me tell you that Mr Perkins is also known as Lord Puzzlewit, and that he can do amazing things with a deck of cards. When performing, Mr Stone is Bondini, Escape Artist Extraordinaire. Chains, locks—nothing can prevent his getting out!"

"Except his wife, of course," put in Mr Perkins, with a wink.

"Just for that," said Mr Stone, "I'm gonna tell the others next time I see you to pull a couple of aces out of your sleeve!"

They all laughed again, making Lewis feel more at ease.

"Well, Lewis, you have a number of experts here," said Mr Hardwick. "So what will it be, gents?"

"The Square Circle," Mr Mussenberger said at once. "You can't go wrong with that."

Mr Perkins stroked his long chin thoughtfully. "Hmm. Perhaps the Linking Rings? Or the Floating Lady? Those both require a lovely assistant."

"The Basket of Torment," added Mr Stone. "Kids, you'll wow 'em. Miss Rose Rita climbs into the basket, Lewis pierces it with a dozen razor-sharp swords, and when the swords are removed, Rose Rita comes out in a completely different costume!"

Mr Hardwick held up his hands. "Please, please! Gentlemen, remember that Lewis and Rose Rita have to be ready in four weeks—and they can't afford fancy props." He got up and opened a door, beckoning Lewis and Rose Rita over. "I'll tell you what. In this room is my collection of books on magic—more than seven thousand of them!" He switched on the light.

Lewis and Rose Rita stepped into a room that was like a library, with shelf after shelf of books. Daylight poured in through two round side windows, and dust motes floated in the slanting sunbeams. Mr Hardwick pointed to a tall bookcase. "Now, this section has all sorts of books on simple stage-magic tricks," he said. "You two rummage around and find five or six likely books, and I'll let you borrow them—if you promise to take very good care of them!"

"We will," Lewis agreed at once.

"Good," Mr Hardwick said. "Now I'll get back to fleecing these three marks. I'm already ahead twenty-five cents!" He closed the door as the others protested against being called "marks."

For a couple of minutes Rose Rita and Lewis just stared at all the books. Then they began to look at the intriguing titles—*Chemical Magic with Everyday Ingredients*; *Close-Up Tricks with Matches, Coins, and String*; *How to Amaze Your Friends*, and others. Lewis pulled some out, thumbed through them, replaced a few, and kept others. At last he clutched five books under his arm. He looked up and saw that Rose Rita was far off at another shelf. "We can't take those," he said.

"I know," replied Rose Rita. "I was just looking. There are books here by Houdini, the great escape artist. And here's one by Blackstone—I've seen him on TV. Here's something funny."

Slapping book dust off his clothes, Lewis went over to look. Rose Rita held a scroll—a rolled-up length of parchment. It had a faded cloth wrapper, and some words had been embroidered on the cloth. Rose Rita read them aloud: "Madame Frisson: Her Testament from Beyond the Grave."

Lewis's neck felt prickly. "I don't think we should mess with that," he said uneasily.

"Don't be such a worrywart. I'm not messing with it—I'm just reading it. What's this?" Rose Rita had found a little pocket in the cloth wrapper. She pulled out a yellowed packet made of paper. Tucking the scroll beneath her arm, she began to unfold the packet as Lewis looked on with a strange dread.

"What is it?" he asked, his voice a dry croak.

"Some kind of grey powder," Rose Rita said. "There's only a teaspoonful of it—Ouch!" She jerked her hand, dropping the packet. It landed flat without spilling much of the powder.

"What's wrong?" Lewis asked, so frightened he almost dropped his books.

"Paper cut." Rose Rita shook her finger, making a face. She reached down to pick up the packet, and a single bright red drop of blood fell from her finger right into the grey substance.

Lewis gasped. The powder began to boil. It hissed and bubbled. A dull brown vapour rose from it, drifting in strange, stringy wisps, like strands of cobwebs. The whole mass sizzled, the reddish-brown bubbles bursting until it became a seething liquid. Then it shrank into a dark little ball about the size of a pea. It was as black and shiny as a round button made of ebony. Rose Rita paused. "What is that?" she asked. "It looks like a small black pearl." She reached down for it—

And yanked her hand away with a startled shriek! The black ball sprouted spindly legs and scuttled under one of the bookshelves. Lewis uttered one strangled shout. Somehow, with Rose Rita's drop of blood, the powder had become a living spider!

CHAPTER THREE

Lewis and Rose Rita backed away towards the door. With his left hand Lewis clutched the books. Reaching behind him with his right, he fumbled for the knob. A horrible thought hit him. What if his hand closed on a cold, squashy, wriggling, round body? Spiders were venomous. He had heard of people dying in agony from the bite of a black widow. The dusty, book-scented air seemed hard to breathe in. His throat closed. Lewis gritted his teeth to keep them from chattering. The spider couldn't be there, he told himself. He had seen it run under a shelf all the way across the room, and it was too small to have zipped past them.

More afraid of what he had seen run under the bookshelf than what might be behind him, Lewis grabbed the knob and opened the door. He and Rose Rita stumbled out. The magicians hardly glanced up from their game. "Find some stuff?" Mr Hardwick asked in a vague kind of tone as he frowned at his cards. He waved a hand. "Fine! Just let yourselves out, and the door will lock behind you. When you finish with the books, bring them back."

Rose Rita rushed for the stairs, and Lewis followed close at her heels. The two of them clattered down the steps. She unlocked the door, and they plunged out into the morning sunlight. The door slammed shut behind them, the automatic lock clicking. For a second Lewis and Rose Rita just stood there looking at each other with wild eyes and panting to get their breath back.

Then the ordinary Saturday-morning sounds of New Zebedee brought them back to reality. Chevrolets and Fords rolled past. Someone's big brown Labrador dog was barking at a frisky squirrel outside the post office. A kid rode his bike down the street, jangling the bell. Lewis took a long, shaky breath, feeling relief at their escape. Then he stared at what Rose Rita held clenched under her arm. "You've still got it!" he said in a shocked voice.

Rose Rita took the scroll in both hands and swallowed hard. In the sunlight it looked worn and shabby. Lewis saw that the scroll itself was parchment or something like it, creased, dull brown, and badly frayed at the edges. It was on a wooden roller like a spool. The cloth covering was moth-eaten purple velvet, faded to a dull brownish maroon. The embroidered letters were a dull greenish yellow. Maybe they had been gold at one time. "I was so scared, I didn't even drop it," Rose Rita said. She looked at Lewis with a sick expression. "What should I do?"

"Give it back to Mr Hardwick," Lewis told her.

Rose Rita bit her lip. She looked from Lewis to the door and then she shook her head. "The door locked behind us. I'd have to knock. He might get mad."

"Why would he get mad?" Lewis asked.

Rose Rita gave him a pained look. "Because he might think I started to swipe it and then lost my nerve. This looks old—it must be valuable."

Lewis took a deep breath. "Maybe we can sneak it back in when we return the books. There's tons of stuff on those shelves. Mr Hardwick probably won't miss one little scroll for a week or so."

"What if he does?" moaned Rose Rita. "Lewis, this isn't like those books you have. This scroll has some kind of real magic about it. I don't like it."

Lewis nodded unhappily. He didn't like real magic either. Not unless his uncle or Mrs Zimmermann was firmly in control of it. Real magic could be unpredictable and deadly. "What's wrong?" Lewis asked, noticing Rose Rita staring at her right index finger.

"This is where I cut myself," Rose Rita said, holding her finger up so he could see it. There was a tiny curved white mark on it, like a quarter moon with its points facing downwards.

Lewis's flesh crawled. He hated cuts and puncture wounds, and he had a morbid fear of getting a deadly infection from one. He asked, "Does it hurt?"

Rose Rita shook her head. "It feels sort of cold. Anyway, it isn't bleeding." She rubbed the scar with her thumb and made a face. "And it doesn't solve my problem with this scroll."

Lewis thought for a minute. Now that they were safely outside, he began to wonder if they'd really seen what they thought they had. Maybe the spider had just been hiding inside the scroll and had dropped out. Maybe the powder had been just something that fizzed when it got wet. Still, Lewis knew you should never take chances where magic might be concerned. "Look," he said, "why don't you let Mrs Zimmermann have a look at the scroll? She'd probably know what to do with it."

"And have her think I was poking my nose in where it didn't belong?" asked Rose Rita fiercely. "Mrs Zimmermann is my best grown-up friend. She'd think I was awful if I told her what I did."

With a sigh Lewis said, "I guess I understand. Maybe you can just put it away until next weekend. We'll try to sneak it back in then. OK?"

"OK," Rose Rita said at last. "I don't like it, but I can't think of anything else. Maybe Mr Hardwick won't miss it. But I still feel like a thief."

"You're not *stealing* it," Lewis pointed out. "You're just borrowing it for a while. And you're not even going to read it."

"You can say that again," Rose Rita told him.

They stopped at Rose Rita's house, and she dashed inside for a few minutes. When she came out, she said, "I hid it in my room. I don't even want to think about it until we can smuggle it back into the museum. Come on. Let's go to your house and try to concentrate on getting our act ready."

At 100 High Street, Lewis and Rose Rita sat at the study table and leafed through the books. They found some pretty good tricks. Finally they agreed that four of them might be easy enough to work out. One was a way to produce a live rabbit or dove from a crumpled-up sheet of newspaper. Another was a trick that would let Lewis seem to levitate Rose Rita. Covered with a sheet, she would appear to rise and float in the air. Actually, she would be holding a pair of fake legs and feet stretched out in front of her. If they could find a couple of big crates or cardboard boxes, there was another neat trick that would let Rose Rita vanish from one and appear in the other. Finally, with the help of a mirror, a chair, and a sword, they could make Rose Rita's head appear to hover in mid-air, unattached to her body.

"Can we get all that stuff?" Rose Rita asked.

"I think so," said Lewis. "I don't know about rabbits or doves, but some of the kids live on farms. Maybe I could borrow a baby chick or duckling. That should work just as well. We can make the fake legs from some of your old jeans, some broomsticks, and an old pair of shoes. Uncle Jonathan can probably find us some big boxes. I know he'll let us borrow his grandfather's Civil War sword, and Mrs Zimmermann has all kinds of mirrors in her house." Lewis thought he might talk his uncle into getting him a special outfit too. A tuxedo, maybe. Rose Rita could wear a costume too. They discussed what would be best—maybe a tuxedo for girls. "We'll need two pairs," Rose Rita pointed out. "One for me, one for the fake legs."

They worked everything out. By the time Rose Rita left, Lewis was feeling better. The shock of the spider's appearance had worn off, the two of them had solved the problem of the talent show, and things were looking up. Or so he thought.

When Rose Rita headed home, she walked slowly and thoughtfully. She kept rubbing her thumb over the white scar on her finger. It felt cold and numb. The day was cold too, and though a bright sun shone, to Rose Rita it seemed as if a veil had fallen, dimming the clear blue sky, cooling the September sunlight. She had the strangest feeling of not being quite *there*, as if she were only dreaming about walking home. Her mood was dark also. Rose Rita hated junior high. The other girls talked about only one topic: boys, boys, boys. Some of them made fun of her for hanging out with Lewis, who was short, chunky, and no good at sports. Rose Rita knew that the other girls made catty remarks about her. Behind her back they called her "beanpole" or "four-eyes."

It wasn't fair. Just because she had been born with long bones, straight hair, and nearsighted eyes, the others acted as if she weren't as human as they were. Sometimes Rose Rita felt all mixed up. The things she had cared about all her life—history and baseball and her friends—now seemed childish and unimportant. Other things, like having gorgeous hair and wearing fabulous dresses, seemed more grown-up. Still, Rose Rita thought the girls who spent all their time mooning over movie actors and singers and kids like Dave Shellenberger were silly.

And as if she didn't have enough on her mind already, the scroll waited in her room at the bottom of her sock drawer. She remembered the sharp pain of the paper cut and the eerie way the spider had come to life. Rose Rita had the uneasy feeling that Lewis was right. She should tell Mrs Zimmermann about the scroll. Mrs Zimmermann would understand—

Ugh! Rose Rita stopped dead in her tracks. She had walked into an invisible spider-web, and it clung to her cheeks. Frantically, she brushed her face to get the sticky strands off. But she couldn't feel anything. Not with her hand, at least.

Yet her mouth felt as if a web had been pulled across it, touching lightly and tickling. Rose Rita began to panic. What if it were some kind of magical web? What if it were connected in some way with the spider? "I won't tell!" she vowed at last, and the feeling eased without quite going away.

Rose Rita hurried the rest of the way home, occasionally swiping at her face with the palm of a hand. She couldn't rub away the sensation. It stayed with her into the evening. After dinner Rose Rita's father, George Pottinger, liked to stretch out in an armchair and listen to a Detroit Tigers baseball game on the radio. Usually Rose Rita joined him, but on this Saturday night she just dragged herself upstairs to her room.

Rose Rita went to bed early. She lay there feeling weary, but she couldn't sleep. She heard the sounds of her mother and father getting ready for bed, and then the house was quiet. Lying there, Rose Rita felt like screaming. No one understood her. Her mum and dad were kind and well-meaning, but they didn't remember what being young was like. They never gave her good answers to her questions.

Mrs Pottinger fussed and fretted, and Mr Pottinger always began, "In *my* day we didn't have that problem."

Uncle Jonathan and Lewis were good friends, but they couldn't know what growing up as an ordinary-looking, even plain girl was like. Mrs Zimmermann always listened sympathetically, but her advice was "Be what you are." That was the problem. Rose Rita wasn't really sure *what* she was, or what she wanted to be. She began to feel sorry for herself. Tears stung her eyes.

Somehow she must have drifted off to sleep at last. She had one of those weird dreams in which she knew she was dreaming. It seemed to Rose Rita that she could fly, and she found herself floating along high above New Zebedee. Below her the town spread out like a scale model of itself, from Wilder Park to the quiet neighbourhoods to the north. The trees were red, yellow, and orange. Traffic crept along. It looked like an ordinary autumn day. She sailed over the junior high and saw a bunch of girls she knew standing outside, laughing and talking. Mischievously, Rose Rita decided to show off her flying talent. She dropped lower and lower over the girls, thinking that it didn't matter if she scared them. This was only a dream, after all, and nothing she did would really hurt them.

As she slipped lower, Rose Rita could hear the girls giggling and screeching and acting silly, the way they always did. A brown-haired girl named Sue Gottschalk said, "She gives me the creeps, that's all. I think she looks like a long, tall bag of bones!"

"No," said Lauren Muller. "She's not a bone—she's the dog!"

They all roared with laughter. Sue said, "That gives me a great idea. My dad's promised me a puppy for my birthday. If it's a girl, I'm going to name it Rose Rita!"

Rose Rita felt her face turn hot and red. They were talking about her! Rose Rita had always thought that some of the girls, such as Sue, were her friends. Now she wanted to shrivel up and die. She wanted to fly to the moon and never come back.

"No," said a strange, breathy voice, a woman's voice. "Running away is no good, not with your powers. Use your strength. Teach these unworthy ones a lesson."

Rose Rita could not see anyone who might have spoken. Twirling slowly in the air, Rose Rita asked, "Who is that?"

"A friend." Now Rose Rita could tell that the voice was in her mind, and not coming from outside. "Drop down, down, and take one of them. Take Sue. That will show them!"

Rose Rita grinned. Yes, that would show them! She'd snatch Sue right off the ground and scare the daylights out of her. Rose Rita began to drop lower, lower, slowly, and then she stretched out her long, shiny, hairy arms—

Eight of them!

Rose Rita looked down at herself and screamed in terror. She wasn't flying—she was dangling from a spider-web. Her body had become a huge bloated thing, hairy and blue-black and round as a ball. She opened her mouth to scream, and she found she could make only a hissing noise. Thick green venom drooled out of her mouth.

She had become a giant spider!

MADAME FRISSON: HER TESTAMENT FROM BEYOND THE GRAVE

CHAPTER FOUR

Rose Rita woke up panting and thrashing. She threw her covers off and jumped out of bed. She turned on the light. Her familiar room looked the same. Her goldfish swam in their tank; the high, black bureau stood against the wall; her maths homework lay spread out on her desk. And she was her normal, tall, skinny self. Rose Rita was a sensible girl who did not believe in letting something as unreal as a dream bother her. Still, just remembering the nightmare made her shudder with revulsion. Barefooted, she went to the bathroom and got a drink of water. When she returned to her bedroom, she looked at her bedside clock. It was past two in the morning.

"I should be sleepy," Rose Rita muttered. "But now I'm wide awake." She straightened out her sheets and cover. Should she read for a little while and see if that made her sleepy? She had just started a novel by C. S. Forrester about a brave naval captain back in the days of the Napoleonic wars. Rose Rita went to her bureau to get it. Then she remembered the scroll. It lay in the top drawer, just a few inches away from her hand. Slowly, as if her hand had a mind of its own, it pulled the drawer open. The scroll was there, along with her miniature Little Duke playing cards, her set of Drueke chessmen, and a little carved wooden farmhouse-and-barn set that Mrs Zimmermann had bought for her during a trip to Pennsylvania. Rose Rita didn't plan to take the scroll out. She just wanted to look at it, to make sure it was still there.

Somehow, though, Rose Rita found herself back in bed, with pillows propped up behind her. She carefully removed the rolled-up scroll from its cloth wrapper. Like Lewis, Rose Rita had decided that the spider might have just been hiding in the scroll. She didn't want another ugly surprise like that. The parchment felt soft, dusty, and leathery. Rose Rita unrolled it a little. The edges were frayed and worn, but the scroll was not too badly damaged. A peculiar, musty, spicy scent rose from the old parchment. It was not unpleasant, but it seemed a little unsettling. Rose Rita unwound more of the scroll, revealing lettering.

It looked like handwriting. Maybe the ink once had been black and bold, but time had faded it to a dreary, dull brown, almost the colour of dried blood. Rose Rita blinked at the strange phrases:

THE LAST TESTAMENT OF BELLE FRISSON,

The Greatest Sorceress of Her Age

Reading this gave Rose Rita a strange feeling. She remembered Mr Hardwick's sign in the window of the magicians' museum. The words were obvious exaggerations—they were kind of funny. Mr Hardwick's sign had the humour of a tall tale. But the heading on the scroll didn't seem funny at all. Whoever Belle Frisson was, Rose Rita thought, she had actually believed herself to be the greatest sorceress of her age. Suddenly the night outside seemed darker. Anything might be waiting out there beyond her closed window. Peering in at her. Watching her.

"Oh, get a grip," Rose Rita told herself. She thrust the scroll back into its cover and under the socks again. Climbing back into bed, she lay awake for a long time. Finally she slipped into an uneasy sleep. Vague dreams made her toss and turn, but she did not wake up again until morning.

For the rest of the week Rose Rita and Lewis practised every day after school. Lewis would be the star of the first trick. And later Rose Rita would take centre stage for a trick of her own. Lewis and Rose Rita would come out onstage, and he would introduce them both. Then she would pick up a sheet of newspaper from a low platform on the stage. Rose Rita would display the newspaper, holding it so the audience could see both the front and the back. Then she would fold it again and hand it to Lewis.

Lewis would take the newspaper and hold it up, open it wide, and say a magic word. Then he would crumple the paper into a ball. He would tear away the paper, like someone peeling an orange, and the live dove—except it would be a chick or duckling—would peep out. At least that was the way the trick was supposed to work. In their rehearsals Lewis had no live animal.

Instead, Lewis practised until he could successfully produce his stand-in chick, one of his uncle's white socks, stuffed with more socks. Doing the trick really wasn't too hard. As the magic book explained, the key to sleight of hand is misdirection. That meant Lewis had to make the audience suspect the trick was in one part of the presentation, when it really was elsewhere. In this case the audience would be looking closely at the newspaper as Rose Rita paraded back and forth, opening it, showing both sides, even shaking it. The newspaper was not gimmicked, however.

The real trick was that Lewis had made a sort of cloth swing from a handkerchief and some strong black thread. While Rose Rita was showing the paper, Lewis would hook two loops of the black thread around his right thumb. He gently held the handkerchief, in which the stuffed sock rested, against his side with his right elbow. His robe would cover it. When Lewis spread the paper wide, he moved his elbow away from his side, and the sock swung out. The open sheet of paper concealed it from the audience. Lewis crushed the paper carefully around it. Then, as he held up the ball of newspaper, he slipped his thumb out of the string. When he tore away the paper and took out the imitation chick, he left the handkerchief and the black string in the ball of paper. The audience would be so surprised at the appearance of the living bird that they wouldn't even think about the paper any more. At least, that was what the book promised.

When Lewis and Rose Rita had practised several times, they showed their presentation to Uncle Jonathan, who laughed when he saw one of his old socks magically come out of the newspaper. "I guess I'm lucky you didn't decide to produce my underwear!" he said with a grin.

Lewis, who was wearing his bathrobe as a substitute for his costume, snickered. "It's supposed to be a chick," he explained.

"Well, you could certainly have fooled me," said Uncle Jonathan. "Rose Rita, you did a great job of showing off the newspaper. I was sure the trick would be to rig it up somehow."

"Thanks," replied Rose Rita.

Lewis looked at her uneasily. Rose Rita had been acting funny all week, dreamy and lost.

Her mind seemed to be miles away. Yet she did just as well at school as she always did, and she certainly didn't mess up the magic act.

On Wednesday they went over to Mrs Zimmermann's house. Mrs Zimmermann was sewing their costumes for them. Lewis would wear a silvery top hat with a big peacock plume in the front; a short velvet cape, black on the outside and lined with purple; a loose purple shirt; and loose scarlet trousers. Mrs Zimmermann was even sewing covers for his shoes from the same silvery material as his hat. It would look as if he were wearing silver shoes. Rose Rita would have on a purple outfit that left her arms bare. Baggy trousers, plus golden shoes, completed the costume. Mrs Zimmermann was also preparing a hairband for Rose Rita, made up of fake pearls strung on a netting of gold-coloured thread.

"You're going to look like true mystics," Mrs Zimmermann told them with a grin after she had finished measuring and sketching. She was a good artist, and she showed them pictures of the way they would look in the costumes. As a reward for their patience Mrs Zimmermann had served up some of her wonderful chocolate-chip cookies and milk. Munching a cookie, Lewis asked that the cape be cut a little fuller, so that he could hide his chick under it for the first trick. Rose Rita just looked at the pictures and nodded. She didn't touch her cookies and milk. Mrs Zimmermann's expression became a little concerned. "Are you feeling all right, Rose Rita?" she asked.

Rose Rita's face flushed. "I wish everybody would stop worrying about me," she snapped. "My mum thinks there's something wrong, Lewis keeps looking at me as if he thinks I'm going to roll over and die, and now you. I'm fine!"

Mrs Zimmermann stared in astonishment. "Good heavens, Rose Rita! Don't bite my head off."

Rose Rita looked at her feet. "I'm sorry," she mumbled. "I'm tired, that's all."

Later, after Rose Rita had left for home, Lewis

asked Mrs Zimmermann, "Do you think she's sick or something?"

Mrs Zimmermann began to fold the cloth that she had spread out on the table. She looked thoughtful and tapped her chin with her finger. "I don't know," she said slowly. "Rose Rita certainly doesn't seem to be her usual lively self, but she's at an awkward age for a girl. She's having strange feelings that she never had before. And she's always been very self-conscious. I wouldn't be surprised if the other girls in school are making fun of her."

That upset Lewis. "Why would they do that? She's great!"

Mrs Zimmermann shrugged and gave Lewis a sad smile. "You know that and I know that, Lewis, but Rose Rita isn't so sure. When you're a little different from all the others, they tend to pick on you. I don't suppose Rose Rita's classmates are intentionally cruel, but some girls can be thoughtless. Rose Rita is lucky to have a good friend like you. I think she'll come through all the stress and strain very well, but you'll have to let her feel sad and mopey every once in a while. Now, then: do you want silver bells on your shoes, or will they be all right just plain?"

By the following Saturday Lewis had carefully copied all the directions for their four tricks. After breakfast he headed downtown to return the books. It was a cool morning. Autumn was definitely on the way. Lewis wore his jacket over a red-plaid flannel shirt, but he still felt chilly when the wind blew in his face. He hurried down the hill and met Rose Rita at her house. She was wearing a baggy Notre Dame jacket that had belonged to her uncle. "Got it?" asked Lewis.

Rose Rita nodded and unzipped the jacket. Inside she had concealed the scroll. "I'll be glad to get rid of this thing," she murmured.

Lewis could only agree. Rose Rita looked terrible. Her eyes had dark circles under them, and they held a strange, haunted, anxious expression. She looked thinner too. The two friends walked downtown without saying anything to each other.

Their timing was perfect. They met Mr Hardwick outside the National Museum of Magic just as he fitted his key into the lock. He looked up and smiled. "Lewis and Rose Rita! What a pleasure to see you again. Want me to take those?"

"No," said Lewis quickly. "We'll put them back for you."

Mr Hardwick opened the door. "In we go! Thanks, Lewis. That's very considerate of you. I hope you found some good tricks."

"We did," replied Lewis. "We're going to have a great act."

Rose Rita, who had not said a word for many minutes, suddenly blurted out, "Mr Hardwick, who was Belle Frisson?"

Mr Hardwick switched on the lights, then turned and gave her a quizzical look. "Why, where did you hear that name? I didn't think anyone remembered her."

"Umm," said Lewis, "she was mentioned in one of the old books."

Mr Hardwick nodded and adjusted his glasses. "Let me see, what do I remember about Belle Frisson?" He clicked his tongue a couple of times. "Hmm. Well, to begin with, her real name was Elizabeth Proctor. Do you two know anything about the Fox sisters?"

When both Lewis and Rose Rita shook their heads, Mr Hardwick said, "Come on upstairs, and I'll tell you about them." They followed him. He turned on the lights there too and told them to sit down. They sat in the comfortable chairs arranged around the card table. Mr Hardwick said, "You have to understand that the Fox sisters were quite a sensation hundreds of years ago. It began in Hydesville, New York, in 1848. Maggie and Katie Fox were fifteen and twelve years old. They claimed they started to hear strange thumping noises at night. Do you know what a poltergeist is?"

Again Lewis shook his head, but Rose Rita said, "It's some kind of ghost, isn't it?"

"Absolutely right," said Mr Hardwick. "The word is German and means 'noisy ghost.' Well,

Maggie and Katie said they began to ask this thumping spirit questions, and it answered with one rap for *yes* and two for *no*. Later they worked out an alphabet code too. Their older sister Leah joined in, and the girls began to attract attention as spirit mediums. They would have séances, and the spirits of the dead would supposedly answer their questions. They became world famous. Eventually Elizabeth Proctor saw them perform. She was an unsuccessful actress at the time. She went back to her hometown of Savannah, Georgia, and put together a magic act that she claimed was based on ancient Egyptian sorcery. It was full of fake poltergeist phenomena. This time she succeeded. From about 1855 to the time she died in 1878, she toured the country as Belle Frisson."

Rose Rita frowned. "She didn't deal with real ghosts?"

Mr Hardwick guffawed. "Well, neither did the Fox sisters," he said. "In time they confessed it was all trickery. Lots of people believed that Belle Frisson had real magic power, but I'm sure it was all just part of the act. I think I've got a book that has a chapter on her. The writer halfway believed in her powers, so you have to take what he says with a grain of salt." Pausing, Mr Hardwick looked thoughtful. "You know, you could visit Belle Frisson's grave if you wanted. She's buried only about twenty miles from here, in a cemetery just outside of Cristobal."

"Where's that?" Lewis asked.

"Oh, it's a small farm village southwest of here," Mr Hardwick said. "That little cemetery is quite unusual. It has half a dozen magicians buried in it." He got up. "Let me find your book, and you can replace the ones you borrowed."

They went into the next room, and Lewis began to put the books back on the shelves. Mr Hardwick climbed up on a ladder and reached above his head for a volume, and as he did, Rose Rita quickly took the scroll from her jacket and shoved it back into its place, in an open-topped box. She jerked her hand away quickly. Something had popped up from the box as Rose Rita replaced the scroll. It was a big black spider, its body as large as a grape. It raised its two front legs threateningly, then darted behind the rows of books. Rose Rita looked at Lewis with wide, sick eyes.

"Here we are," Mr Hardwick said cheerfully, stepping down from the ladder. He held a worn old book, bound in deep olive-green leather. He handed it over to Rose Rita. "Be careful with this," he said. "It was published in Chicago in 1885. It's quite rare."

"I'll be careful," promised Rose Rita. She took the book from Mr Hardwick and thanked him, and then she and Lewis left. On the pavement outside, Rose Rita said, "Whew! I'm glad that's all over."

"So am I," said Lewis. He glanced anxiously at Rose Rita. She still looked tired and drawn, and she had pulled her head down low because of the chilly wind. She held the old volume tight against her chest. Lewis wondered if it really *was* over—if whatever had been bothering

Rose Rita was somehow tied in with Belle
Frisson, the scroll, and the mysterious spider.
He hoped that whatever they had started would
end now. Maybe replacing the scroll would
break whatever weird chain of events they had
accidentally begun.

But he had his doubts.

CHAPTER FIVE

September passed. October began, with cool, crisp days filled with the scent of burning leaves. Rose Rita and Lewis practised and practised until they could do all four magic tricks perfectly. There was only one problem. Lewis still had not been able to rehearse the newspaper stunt with a live animal. "Maybe you could produce a bouquet of flowers instead of a chick," suggested Uncle Jonathan a couple of days before the talent show.

Lewis shook his head impatiently. In some

ways Lewis was a real perfectionist. Some things had to be done just right, or they were no good at all, and the magic trick was one of them. He said, "Flowers wouldn't be the same. Timmy Lindholm's going to bring a chick in for me. It'll be all right." And he really thought it would. He had become very adept at swinging the stuffed sock into the newspaper without anyone seeing the move. Even Mrs Zimmermann, who had sharp eyes for foolery, couldn't quite tell how he produced the sock from the balled-up newspaper.

In fact, Lewis would have been very happy except for his continuing worries about Rose Rita. It was not that she had changed, exactly. She still practised with him, she tried on the costume that Mrs Zimmermann had made, and she went to school every day, the same as always. But Rose Rita had become even more withdrawn, silent, and absent recently. She went through their magic routine as if she had only half her mind on what she was doing. At school Rose Rita hardly talked to anyone. She hurried

67

away from the little groups of girls that gathered on the playground or stood outside near the steps. In class she responded when the teachers called on her, but she stopped raising her hand to answer questions.

Lewis found that especially unusual. Rose Rita always waved her hand eagerly when the teacher asked something she knew. He also missed her elaborate tales. Rose Rita had once told him she wanted to be a famous writer when she grew up, and she certainly had the imagination. Often she would dream up some outrageous or funny story about their teachers or classmates and spin it out for Lewis with a straight face. She might tell how Bill Mackey, an annoying, gangly kid with big feet, had been kidnapped by Martians when he was a baby and raised on Mars. Since the gravity there is low, Rose Rita would explain, Bill grew to be a beanpole. The Martians brought him back when they discovered he was a human. They had wanted a pet animal and had made a natural mistake.

Rose Rita had lots of wild stories like that one, but even though Lewis encouraged her to tell him one, she refused. Unlike Rose Rita, Lewis could never decide what he wanted to be when he grew up. Sometimes he thought it would be fun to be a photographer for *National Geographic* and go all over the globe taking pictures of dusty herds of elephants and lofty snowcapped mountains. At other times he wanted to be an airline pilot, a research chemist, or an astronomer. Usually he could tease Rose Rita into making up a story about what life would be like if he were photographing crocodiles on the banks of the Nile or bending over a telescope on Mount Palomar, searching the night sky for comets. Lately, however, she didn't even seem to listen to him.

The week of the talent show was so hectic that Lewis almost forgot to worry about Rose Rita. For many years the junior-high students had performed the show in the school cafeteria. This year they would put it on in the municipal auditorium, the refurbished New Zebedee

Opera House. Lewis had bad memories of that stage, and just standing on it made him nervous, but all the kids would have to perform there. The teachers had planned the talent show for the evening of 9th October, a Friday. On Thursday afternoon they all had a dress rehearsal in the auditorium.

The New Zebedee Opera House was an old theatre in the top two stories of the Farmers' Feed & Seed building. It had a horseshoe-shaped balcony, rows of red velvet-covered seats, and an ornate stage. The walls had been painted pink, with intricate designs in gold framing the stage. On one side was the grieving theatrical mask of tragedy, and on the other the laughing mask of comedy. Uncle Jonathan helped Lewis carry all his magical paraphernalia upstairs and put it out of the way backstage. The two of them had found two big cardboard boxes, which Lewis and Rose Rita had painted with tempera. One was red and yellow, and the other blue and purple. Rose Rita would climb into the red-and-yellow one, and after some hocus-pocus on Lewis's part she would reappear in the blue-and-purple one. They also hauled up a sort of low sofa that Uncle Jonathan had knocked together from some scrap lumber, some cotton stuffing, and some upholstery material. It had casters so that it could roll on and off the stage, and Rose Rita would lie on it before the levitation stunt. Finally, they brought up the chair and the mirror for the last trick, the one in which Rose Rita's head would seem to float in mid-air.

As rehearsal began, Lewis got into his costume and paced around backstage while Dave Shellenberger and Tom Lutz practised their comedy act. They were imitating the famous comedians Bud Abbott and Lou Costello doing a baseball skit called "Who's on first?" The other kids stood in the wings listening and laughing their heads off, but Lewis was too tense to watch. He saw James Gensterblum tuning up his guitar. James was wearing a grey-and-black striped shirt and grey trousers, and his blue eyes were narrowed in concentration.

"Hey, James," Lewis whispered, "have you seen Timmy around?"

James shook his head. "Not since we left school. He should be here, though. He's gonna juggle."

For a few minutes Lewis watched James lower his head over his guitar and listen carefully as he tuned.

"Hey, Lewis," James said suddenly. "Timmy just came in."

Lewis looked in the direction James pointed. Timmy, an easygoing, tubby boy with curly black hair and a freckled nose, came backstage. He lugged a canvas bag, which he set down in a corner. Lewis hurried over to him, asking, "Did you bring it?"

Timmy sighed. "Aw, gee, I forgot, Lewis. I'm sorry."

"I need that chicken," said Lewis, annoyed at Timmy's absentmindedness.

"I'll get one for you. I just forgot." Timmy took some bowling-pin-shaped clubs from his bag. He rolled up the sleeves of his blue shirt. "I gotta practise now."

Lewis frowned as Timmy began to toss and catch the three clubs. Timmy was pretty good at juggling, but he had a lousy memory.

Rose Rita came out of the girls' dressing room. She had changed into her costume. James and Timmy looked at her and grinned, but she didn't seem to notice them. "You ready?" Lewis asked her.

Rose Rita just nodded.

Their magic act came after Tom and Dave's "Who's on first?" routine. Miss Fogarty, their English teacher, sat in the auditorium, along with Uncle Jonathan and a few parents. One of the parents, Mr Lutz, was helping backstage. He put on a record that Lewis gave him, "Sabre Dance." As soon as the music started, Lewis stepped out from behind the curtains.

Footlights and spotlights shone in his face, dazzling him. He could hardly see anything out in the audience—just the gleam of light reflected in Miss Fogarty's glasses. "Ladies and

73

gentlemen," he said in a squeaky, frightened voice, "I am the Mystifying Mysto, Master of Illusion! Let me introduce you to my beautiful assistant, the Fantastic Fiona!"

Rose Rita came out from the wings holding the newspaper. She went through the act just as they had practised for weeks, and Lewis produced the sock, calling it "a live chick, produced by magic!" He began to feel better when someone, probably his uncle Jonathan, applauded. They did the other tricks without a hitch and then took their bows. The curtain fell, and Lewis and Rose Rita got their stuff offstage with James's help. "That was great," James whispered as Timmy's juggling music began.

"Thanks," Lewis said. He felt drained. Now that his turn was over, his knees began to shake, and he was dizzy. To Rose Rita he said, "I think we've finally got it down."

Rose Rita just shrugged, as if she didn't really care.

Friday was horrible. All day long the talent show tormented Lewis. He hated the thought of going out onstage in front of everyone. Though he tried to tell himself that everything would go well, doubts and fears kept nagging him. He decided that Rose Rita was right. She often called him a worrywart and accused him of always looking on the dark side. Lewis hated when he did that, but he couldn't help himself. Now he kept imagining all kinds of disasters that could happen. Whenever he thought about forgetting his lines or making some stupid mistake, his hands felt cold and his stomach churned. He could not keep his mind on school, and his maths teacher snapped at him, "Lewis, pay attention!"

Lewis wanted to practise after school, but Rose Rita shook her head and drifted away, walking towards home. Lewis slouched along behind her with his hands in his pockets. Because of the talent show none of the teachers had given homework, and he had no books to carry, but he was in a foul mood. Deliberately walking slowly, he watched Rose Rita up ahead. He was beginning to think she wasn't much of a friend. She didn't seem to care about their act enough to practise one last time.

As they headed up Mansion Street, with Lewis fifty feet behind Rose Rita, he felt cold all over. Rose Rita was walking beside the privet hedge in front of Martha Westley's house. The yard was Mrs Westley's pride and joy, and the hedge was neatly trimmed. Lewis squinted. Something dark was creeping along at the base of the hedge, right beside Rose Rita. It looked like a steel-grey kitten or puppy, except that it moved strangely, in jerky darts. It looked more like an impossibly big insect than anything else.

Rose Rita passed the hedge, and the dark blob moved out of its shadow. Lewis's throat was dry. When the shape moved from the shade into the sunshine, it simply vanished, becoming as transparent as a soap bubble. Rose Rita walked on alone. Still, Lewis had a hard time getting his breath. In the single instant before it had disappeared, the shape had looked as if it had long, busy legs and a round, shiny body. It looked like a spider the size of a kitten.

Rose Rita turned at her house and went up the steps and inside. Walking slowly past, Lewis peered this way and that, staring hard at the piles of autumn leaves along the kerb, at the roots of hedges and bushes. He could smell the autumn scent of burning leaves, and he could hear the dry rustling of more leaves overhead. The rustling made him jerk his gaze upwards. What if the sound wasn't just the wind? What if that horrible creature was lurking up there, ready to drop its cold, clutching body on to the back of his neck? Lewis broke into a frantic run. He did not stop until he had slammed the door of his house safely behind him.

Late that afternoon Uncle Jonathan and Lewis piled into Jonathan's big, old-fashioned car, a black Muggins Simoon. They pulled out into the street in a cloud of exhaust fumes and drove to Mansion Street to pick up a glum and withdrawn Rose Rita. Then they drove downtown, where Jonathan found a parking slot near the Feed & Seed store. With his stomach already feeling queasy from stage fright, Lewis climbed out of the car. Mrs Zimmermann had driven in earlier to help prepare the refreshments, and Lewis saw her car parked nearby.

They hurried upstairs. As he headed for the stage, Lewis thought that the mask of tragedy painted on the wall looked just about as upset as he felt. He went to the boys' dressing room and got into his costume. Then he checked all his magic props. Everything was ready. Now if only Timmy would remember to bring the chick, Lewis was all set to go.

Timmy was late, as always. Lewis impatiently paced back and forth backstage, pausing every now and then to part the curtains and peep out at the growing crowd. All the elementary-school kids and their parents were coming in, together with the parents of the performers. Lewis had a big hard lump in his throat that he couldn't seem to swallow. Just the thought of doing his act in front of nearly five hundred people terrified him. His legs felt rubbery and weak, his head spun, and the breath caught in his lungs.

At last Timmy came hurrying down the aisle, carrying two bags. One was his canvas bag of juggling clubs and balls, and the other was a burlap sack. Lewis rushed to meet him. "Hi," said Timmy with a grin as soon as he was backstage. "I brought your chicken." He handed Lewis the burlap bag, which felt surprisingly heavy.

Lewis opened the bag and looked inside. A white hen stared back at him, her head tilted sideways, her little chicken eyes bright. "Timmy!" exploded Lewis. "This is a full-grown chicken!"

Timmy looked confused. "Huh? Didn't you want a chicken? You kept asking me to bring one."

"I wanted a *baby* chick," wailed Lewis. "Not a grown-up hen!"

With a shrug, Timmy said, "Henrietta will be OK. She's a good chicken. She's just like a pet.

You can pick her up and everything. Anyway, you'll have to use her, because I don't have time to go back and get another one. I gotta practise my juggling."

Timmy unpacked his clubs and started tossing them through the air. Lewis found a dark corner. He peered down into the burlap bag uncertainly. Henrietta stared back at him. Lewis was not at all sure that this would work. He wished he had brought a bouquet of flowers along, just in case something like this happened. But since he hadn't, Lewis decided that he'd better practise the trick with Henrietta. Getting one of the sheets of newspaper from the prop table, Lewis hooked the string-and-handkerchief swing around his thumb and then reached into the bag. Henrietta was feathery, soft, and hot. He pulled her out of the bag. She was a very calm chicken. Lewis looped the handkerchief swing around her, so she was sort of lying in it, and tucked her under his robe. It was hard for him to hold her with his elbow, because she was so large and heavy.

Lewis held the newspaper, then spread it out. The swing swooped out from his elbow, he crushed the paper into a loose ball that barely covered Henrietta, and then he tore it away. Henrietta cocked her head this way and that and clucked once. Lewis had been holding his breath. He whooshed it out in relief. Maybe, he thought, the trick was going to work after all.

The talent show began when Miss White, the music teacher, played an overture on the piano and announced to everyone that the junior-high students were pleased to carry on the tradition here in this wonderful new auditorium. Then the curtain went up and the first talent act started. Lewis stood in the wings, watching, with Henrietta tucked beneath his robes and under his arm. Her body heat made him uncomfortably warm, and he started to sweat. Henrietta must have felt hot too, because soon she began to squirm and complain. Rose Rita came over and stood beside Lewis as Tom and Dave did their comedy routine. They wore goofy-looking old-fashioned baseball uniforms, and they had pasted fake moustaches under their noses. They got lots of laughter and applause. Then Miss White said, "Next we have a real treat—a magic act that will leave you baffled and bewildered!" Mr Lutz started "Saber Dance" on the phonograph, and Lewis stumbled out onstage, under the hot glare of the lights.

"Ladies and gentlemen," rasped Lewis. He swallowed and squeaked, "Ladies and gentlemen," again. Taking a deep breath, Lewis blurted, "I am, uh, the Mystifying Mysto, Master of Illusion!"

From beneath his right arm Henrietta commented, "Bu-u-u-u-ck!"

Lewis squeezed the hen a little more securely. He said, "Let me introduce you to my beautiful assistant, the Fantastic Fiona!"

Rose Rita, looking as if she were in a trance, came out from the wings holding the newspaper. Lewis said, "I will ask the Fantastic Fiona to show you, uh, this perfectly, uh, ordinary—" He was really squirming, because Henrietta was trying to escape. He could feel her writhing and kicking, and he held on to her desperately. "This, uh, ordinary newspaper, and then I'll ask her to give it to me right now!" he finished in a rush.

Rose Rita took her time, just as they had rehearsed. Meanwhile, Henrietta was making determined efforts to find a way out from under those hot robes. Lewis felt his face get hot and red as he wriggled and squirmed, trying to control the hen. At last Rose Rita gave him the newspaper. He reached for it with a feeling of relief.

And everyone started to laugh. In a flurry of feathers, Henrietta dropped out from beneath Lewis's robe. She flapped and squawked. Lewis hadn't even started the trick. He stared at Rose Rita, wondering what to do. She just stared back at him. Out in the audience some kid yelled, "Fake!" Other people started to jeer.

Lewis felt panicky. The chicken stood in the spotlight, jerking her head left and right. People were laughing and calling out things like "Why did the chicken cross the road?" and "Which came first, the chicken or the egg?"

Rose Rita gave Lewis a sharp nudge. "Uh, a live chicken, produced by magic," Lewis said lamely. "Now my assistant will lie down on this magic sofa, and we will perform for you the ancient art of levitation." He took Rose Rita's hand and escorted her to the sofa. Everyone was still laughing. Henrietta was pacing back and forth near the front of the stage, emitting long, contented clucks.

Rose Rita lay down, and Lewis picked up the sheet that would cover her. He spread it out, and as he did, Rose Rita moved her own feet down to either side of the low sofa and picked up the fake feet. Trying hard to ignore the chicken, which was sitting in the middle of the stage, Lewis covered Rose Rita and turned to the audience. "Now with the mystic words—"

Henrietta was right beside Lewis. She suddenly stood up, cackling, "Bu-buck! Bu-buck! Bu-buck!" A gleaming white egg rested on the stage. Then people really began to hoot and cheer. More kids were shouting, "Lewis is a fake! Boo-ooo!"

A humiliated Lewis thought he was going to die. He held up his hands, forgot the magic words he was supposed to say, and yelled, "Rise up! Rise up!"

With her back bent and the fake legs held out beneath the sheet, Rose Rita raised herself off the sofa. Usually the illusion looked really good—just as if Rose Rita had mysteriously begun to float a few feet in the air under the sheet. But this time Lewis was distracted, and he did not notice he was standing on a corner of the sheet. When Rose Rita lifted herself up, the sheet fell away, revealing her holding those stupid-looking fake legs.

"It's a trick!" yelled someone in the audience. "Get off the stage! Boo!" Other kids joined in the catcalls. "You're no magician!" "Go back to the farm!" "Take your chicken home and cook it!"

Rose Rita dropped the legs and stood up, her face still burning red. She scowled out at the audience. Now all the elementary-school kids were shrieking, "Boo! Boo!"

Henrietta flapped her wings and cackled again. A single white feather floated in the air, twirling and twisting.

Lewis wanted to shrivel up and creep into a hole somewhere.

And then, to his shock, he heard Rose Rita shout above all the noise, "Shut up! I hate you all! I'm going to make you pay!"

Mercifully, the curtain dropped. Rose Rita turned and glared at Lewis, then stalked away. Lewis thought his heart had stopped.

In that terrifying moment Rose Rita hadn't looked like herself at all. Her eyes had been completely black and glittery, as if they were made up of thousands of facets, like the eyes of a spider. A spider in human form.

CHAPTER SIX

Rose Rita huddled in the smelly dark, seething with anger. She hated Lewis for making her look ridiculous. She hated the school for having the stupid talent contest in the first place. Most of all, she hated the kids and even the grown-ups in the audience who had made fun of her. "I'll make them pay," she growled to herself. She sat in a hunched-up position, hugging her knees. Her hiding place was cramped and hot, but she didn't care. She didn't even care that it smelled bad—mildew and disinfectant and cleaning fluid all mixed together. Rose Rita was trying hard to think up ways of getting back at everyone who had made her a laughing stock.

Someone knocked at the door, making her jump. She bumped her head but bit her lip to keep from yelling and giving herself away. Then she heard Mrs Zimmermann's kindly voice: "Are you in there, Rose Rita?"

"No!" snapped Rose Rita, though she knew how dumb that would sound. "Go away."

"I don't think I should. May I come in?"

Rose Rita didn't say anything. She shrugged in the dark. She should have realised there was no way to hide from Mrs Zimmermann. Mrs Zimmermann had all sorts of spells she could use to find anything lost or in hiding. The doorknob rattled, and Mrs Zimmermann swung open the door of the janitor's closet. She looked down at Rose Rita, who was crouched in the corner under a thick plywood shelf stacked with cans of cleaning products, boxes of lightbulbs and steel wool, and wadded cleaning cloths. Mrs Zimmermann wrinkled her nose as she peered into the darkness. "I might have expected to find you just about anywhere but here. Good heavens, but you picked a smelly place to hide!"

"I don't care," replied Rose Rita grumpily. She was still wearing her costume, though the talent show had ended half an hour earlier. She pulled her legs a little closer, scrunching as far back into her corner as she could.

"Well, if you don't care, then I don't either," said Mrs Zimmermann brightly. She crouched down slowly until she was sitting in the doorway, her legs bent to the side. "What happened up on the stage isn't the end of the world, you know."

"It might as well be for me," grumbled Rose Rita. She punched her glasses back into place on her nose and sniffled a little. After a little while she quietly asked, "Is everyone gone now?"

"Just about," said Mrs Zimmermann. The janitor's closet was at the end of a short hall, where only one dim bulb gave any illumination.

The faint light made Mrs Zimmermann's white hair glow, and it reflected in the lenses of her glasses, making them little white circles. She squirmed, trying to make herself more comfortable. "I told your mother and father that I'd bring you home," she said. "I thought you might like some time to cool off."

Rose Rita took a deep breath, and it caught in her throat. She fought back a sob. "Why does everyone have to be so mean?" she asked in a forlorn voice.

Mrs Zimmermann looked down. She pinched the material of her purple dress and started to pleat it absent-mindedly. "I don't believe they think of themselves as mean," she said slowly. "It's more a case of thank-heavens-it-isn't-me. Everyone has embarrassing moments, Rose Rita. When something especially horrible and embarrassing happens, sometimes people forget how others feel. They see the whole event not as a catastrophe, but as a show meant to entertain them. They also feel relieved that they are not the one who is the centre of attention, so they laugh. I don't think anyone really meant you to take it personally."

"Well, I did." Rose Rita could feel her lower lip trembling. Tears blurred her eyes. "Th-they made f-fun of me!"

Mrs Zimmermann held her arms open, and Rose Rita crept forwards and hugged her. Mrs Zimmermann's dress smelled faintly of peppermint. "There, there," said Mrs Zimmermann gently, patting her shoulder. "They made fun of you, but they didn't really hurt you."

Rose Rita straightened up. Her glasses had fogged up from her hot tears. "Y-yes they did!"

Mrs Zimmermann smiled in a sad kind of way. "Oh, I know they hurt your *feelings*. I know that when they were yelling and booing, they made you feel about six inches tall. And I know that you don't think you can face anyone at school on Monday. Still, people forget, Rose Rita. This reminds me of the time I went to a dance when I was sixteen years old. A handsome fellow named Ben Quacken-Bush asked me to dance. Well, he was rugged but clumsy, and he stepped on the hem of my long skirt with his big black loafers. My skirt fell right down to my ankles. There I was, waltzing with my petticoat showing, for all the world to see. That was really scandalous back then!"

With a weak smile Rose Rita said, "It'd be pretty bad even today."

"Well, I don't know," replied Mrs Zimmermann thoughtfully, a glint in her eye. "It might not attract as much attention nowadays. My legs aren't as shapely as they used to be!"

Despite herself Rose Rita giggled. "What happened next?"

Mrs Zimmermann shrugged. "Everyone laughed at me. At school the girls started calling me horrible names. You can imagine how that made me feel. Still, I got over it, and now I even think that what happened with Ben Quacken-Bush had its funny side. I think in time you'll get over what happened tonight too."

Rose Rita looked down at the dirty floor. In

her secret heart she doubted that she would ever get over being laughed at and booed. She didn't want to say that to Mrs Zimmermann, who was only trying to be kind. "Where's Lewis?" she asked in a small voice.

Mrs Zimmermann smiled. "Jonathan drove him home not long after the two of you came offstage. Lewis is going to have a hard time living this down too, you know."

Rose Rita nodded, though privately she felt as if Lewis were to blame for the whole mess.

"Come on," said Mrs Zimmermann, getting slowly to her feet. "You need to change, and we have to get out of here so they can lock this place up for the night." She held out her hand, and Rose Rita let Mrs Zimmermann help her up. Rose Rita had been hiding in the closet so long that her legs were cramped and stiff. Glumly, she went to the girls' dressing room and changed back into her jeans and sweatshirt. Then she and Mrs Zimmermann went down to Mrs Zimmermann's green Plymouth Cranbrook. Rose Rita carried her costume balled up, and she tossed it into the back seat.

Mrs Zimmermann was quiet on the short drive to Mansion Street. She stopped in front of Rose Rita's house. The porch light was on, its yellow glare making harsh shadows on the lawn. "Don't take your anger out on Lewis," said Mrs Zimmermann softly. "Remember, they were laughing at him too. He feels just as bad as you do. The two of you are friends, and friends have to stick together when bad times come along."

Rose Rita just grunted. She opened the passenger door and got out of the car. For a second she thought about getting her costume, but then she decided she never wanted to see it again. Without even thanking Mrs Zimmermann, Rose Rita slammed the car door and ran across the lawn. The front door was unlocked, and she burst through. From the parlour her mother called, "Rose Rita? Is that you?"

"I'm home," Rose Rita called back, and then she ran upstairs to her room. She locked the door and stood with her back against it. Closing her eyes, Rose Rita imagined seeing the darkened theatre, the white chicken, the white gleaming egg. She thought she could almost hear the sniggers and the cruel laughter. She felt the dull heat of anger rising inside her again. "I'll make them pay," she whispered. She began to plan what she could do to humiliate everyone who had laughed at her.

Rose Rita's mother came to her door and asked if she was all right. "I'm fine," Rose Rita called back. "I'm going to bed."

She changed into pyjamas and turned out the light. Lying in the dark, she thought of the weeks she had spent at Camp Kitchitti-Kippi last summer. Rose Rita despised camp, and she had gone only because Lewis was away at Boy Scout camp. She had felt homesick much of the time. In Rose Rita's opinion the other girls at the camp were silly and irritating, but some activities had been fun. At night as they had sat around the campfire, they had sung all sorts of funny camp songs. Then it didn't matter if her voice was on key or so far off that she couldn't have found the right note with a torch. Sometimes Rose Rita thought of the songs when she was feeling blue, and they usually helped cheer her up. One came to her as she lay in the darkness.

The silly song usually made her smile. But after what she had been through, it seemed to have lost its power. Rose Rita lay awake and angry for hours.

The streetlight outside the house seemed unusually bright that night. Rose Rita stared at the window, and as time went by, the window began to gleam in the silvery light of the foggy streetlamp. Inside her room Rose Rita couldn't really see anything—just black shapes where she knew her chair, desk, and bureau were. Her eyes began to feel heavy, until opening them seemed to be too much effort. Her breathing became slower and slower.

As Rose Rita nodded off, she tried in a dreamy, drifting kind of way to figure out what another dark shape was. She sensed it close by, and she forced her weary eyes open just a fraction to look for it. Yes, the shape was very close. It was tall and next to her bed. It might have been a coat rack with a coat or two hanging on it, except that she did not have one in her bedroom. Whatever it was, the form looked unfamiliar, as if it did not belong, and yet Rose Rita felt no surprise at glimpsing it there. A spicy scent wafted from it, dry and tingling in her nose, a little like sage and a little like cloves. She could have reached out and touched the form—it was that close to her bed—but she felt far too tired.

Instead, Rose Rita closed her eyes again and felt something touch her. The soft, dry hand on her forehead was Mrs Zimmermann's, she thought in drowsy confusion, touching her brow in soft, soothing strokes. "I hate them all," murmured Rose Rita.

"I know you do." The voice was just a breathy whisper, so soft it might have come from inside Rose Rita's head. "Hatred is good. It can make you strong."

"Mmm." Rose Rita felt keenly aware of her breathing, deep and regular. Her body felt as though it were floating on a cloud, billowy and soft.

"Your hatred can grow," said the whispery voice. "It can do your will and be your eyes and ears. You can set it free. I can show you how to send it forth to do your bidding." The dry hand stroked her forehead, soothing and light, barely touching her. "I come from the grave to tell you this."

Cold fingers gripped Rose Rita's heart. Her breath stopped. She struggled to breathe again, but she was paralysed.

"It is airless in the grave, dusty and quiet. And you cannot move, cannot scream. You can only think. Think of the power you possessed once and will possess again. I know!"

Rose Rita felt as if her lungs were about to burst. She was suffocating; she fought for air. But the hand pressed against her forehead, hard, pushing her down, down.

The relentless voice went on: "I bring a gift.

You have been chosen. Feed your hate! Make it strong! Call me back!"

The hand pressed down even harder, and Rose Rita lost consciousness. She tumbled into a terrible nightmare, full of scuttling spiders, sticky webs, and dark, misshapen creatures, partly human and partly animal. Hands that were partly claws tore at her. Faces with black bug eyes, with the grimacing mouths of lions, snarled at her. She heard laughter, mocking and hateful. Then everything grew quiet.

Rose Rita dreamed that she stood before a strange sculpture. It was a many-sided pillar taller than her. On top of the pillar rested a stone ball, pitted and worn—a ball so large that Rose Rita could not have encircled it with her arms. Letters had been carved in the base of the pillar, but because of its shape Rose Rita could not read them. She circled the sculpture, trying to follow one line of letters and make sense of them, but they were a jumble.

"Find me," said the breathy, whispery voice

she had heard in her bedroom. "Come and free me."

Rose Rita looked around, but she could see no one. The dark ground stretched bare all the way to the horizon. The world might have been flat, with the sculpture at the very centre. "Where are you?" Rose Rita called, her voice lost and tiny in the vast world.

"Find me," repeated the voice.

Rose Rita turned back to the sculpture. She gazed at the stone ball. Was it turning, slowly rotating? She couldn't be sure. For a long time she watched it. It was like staring at the minute hand of a clock, trying to see whether it was moving or not. Standing on her tiptoes, Rose Rita reached up to touch the strange dark-grey sphere. The stone felt rough and cold beneath her palm.

And then something happened.

Two eyes opened. Eyes in the solid stone.

They stared at Rose Rita with a deep, piercing glare of hatred, looking so evil that Rose Rita gasped.

And then a stone hand emerged from the sphere near the eyes. It seized Rose Rita's hand and froze around it. The grip was solid, cold, rough, and unforgiving. Rose Rita tried to pull away. She could not budge an inch.

Rose Rita stared in horror. Her arm was turning grey and brittle. In a terrible wave, moving past her elbow to her shoulder, her body was changing.

Her flesh was turning to stone.

CHAPTER SEVEN

The next week passed as if Rose Rita had never awakened from that terrible nightmare. She almost felt that she really had been turned to stone. At least, her feelings were as cold as stone. She went to school every day. The other girls talked about her and giggled. Rose Rita ignored them. Lewis, who was suffering from merciless teasing himself, tried to apologise to her. She looked at him as though he were a mile away and didn't say anything. When the teachers gave assignments, Rose Rita did them automatically, like a machine. She didn't speak to anyone—not her mother or father, not Mrs Zimmermann—about the hot little flame of hatred deep down inside her. It seemed to Rose Rita that the angry feeling was the only thing human about her, and she greedily kept it going. Lewis invited her to his house for dinner a couple of times, but Rose Rita just shook her head. She was waiting for something—she did not know what it might be—but somehow she knew that if she talked and laughed with her friends, her precious hot flame of hatred might die. So she kept to herself more than ever, biding her time.

On the Monday afternoon ten days after the talent show, Rose Rita came home from school and found a basket of newly laundered clothes in her room. She began to put them away. She hung blouses and skirts in her closet. She put folded jeans on a shelf. And then she began to match her socks into pairs. Rose Rita opened her bureau drawer and saw something sticking out from under the socks. Something that looked like faded purple velvet. Frowning, Rose Rita burrowed down and came up with the scroll.

"I put this back," muttered Rose Rita, turning the worn velvet cover this way and that. "I know I put this back in the museum."

She trembled, feeling the skin on her arms break out in goosebumps. From deep inside her mind came again a sinister, whispery voice: *I bring a gift. You have been chosen.* Rose Rita watched her hands pull the brittle old scroll from its cover. She felt she had no control over them. Her fingers unrolled the scroll as if someone else were making them move. She scanned the crumply tan-coloured scroll that bore letters and figures drawn in ink that had once been black but over the years had faded to a rusty iron shade. Before, Rose Rita had read only the first part of the scroll, which said that it was the final testament of Belle Frisson. Now she was looking at the rest. It made no sense.

The marks were not letters or numbers or

even pictures, but just random-seeming strokes. Some of them led right off the top edge of the scroll, and others off the bottom. More nonsense chicken scratches covered the middle. Rose Rita had learned a little about foreign languages in school. She could read some Latin and French. In her schoolbooks she had seen reproductions of Egyptian hieroglyphs, Chinese pictographs, and other kinds of writing. The marks on the scroll did not look like any of them. They looked closer to Hebrew or Arabic than anything else, but Rose Rita did not think they were in either of those languages. She continued to unroll the scroll until she came to the very end, and then she gasped.

She saw something she recognised. She had seen it before in her nightmare: a many-sided pillar crowned with a huge ball. Rose Rita's hands began to shake as she remembered the awful feeling of turning into stone. She hastily rolled the scroll back up and thrust it into its cover. Something moved in her room, just at the corner of her vision. Rose Rita whirled. Did a dark shadow, the size of a small dog, dart into her closet? She could not be sure. Rose Rita dropped the scroll on to her bed and reached for her desk chair.

Holding it the same way a lion tamer holds a chair to ward off the dangerous big cats, Rose Rita threw her closet door wide open. Her clothing hung there. Nothing moved. She saw no shadowy shape. However, on the floor of the closet lay the old green book she had borrowed from Mr Hardwick at the museum. With everything that had happened, Rose Rita had not even looked at it. She set the chair down and picked up the old volume. Its leather cover felt pebbly and strangely slick. Rose Rita sat on the edge of her bed and opened the book and read the title page:

Forty Dears Among the Magicians
or,
Friends, the Fakirs, the Fakers,
and the Fabulous Frauds

by Joseph W. Winston,
Stage Manager, Director, and
Theatrical Producer
The Leaoitt Press, Inc.
Chicago, Illinois, 1885

Rose Rita turned a few pages and then began to read what Mr Winston had to say about magicians:

Stage conjurors are among the cleverest people on earth. They delight in controlled confusion, misdirection, and wonderful sleights that deceive us and delight us. Time after time I have witnessed some seeming miracle and have been utterly baffled, only to learn later of the absurdly simple means the artist has used to create the illusion of the miracle. I must admit to curiously mixed feelings in such cases, for part of me is delighted at the cleverness of the performer, whilst another part is annoyed at my own credulity and lack of observation.

And yet, on a few memorable occasions in my four decades of travelling from theatre to theatre, often in the company of such wonder workers, I have encountered what just possibly might be the real thing. Does magic truly exist? Reader, I will leave the question to you. I intend only to bear witness to the half dozen or so performers whose tricks I could never fathom, whose sleights I could never penetrate. Were they tricksters only, or were they perhaps masters of powers most of us cannot even imagine? You be the judge.

Rose Rita turned more pages. She found a whole long chapter headed "BELLE FRISSON: OR, SPEAKING TO THE SPIRITS." Before reading it, Rose Rita stopped at an old-fashioned steel engraving, all dark cross-hatched lines. It showed a woman with a thin, oval face, large, piercing, dark eyes, and jet-black hair. She wore an Egyptian headband with a round medallion in front, and on the medallion was an engraving of a spider. Her sombre eyes seemed to stare right into Rose Rita's. Rose Rita turned the page very quickly.

And then she stared at another picture, a grainy photograph this time. It showed a flat cemetery with headstones crowded thick. At the centre of the picture was a monument far taller than the stones around it. Rose Rita had seen it before. It was the many-sided pillar with the stone ball on top. The caption of the photograph read,

"Belle Frisson, née Elizabeth Proctor, lies buried beneath this strange monument. People report that the ball slowly revolves, with no visible power. Does her spirit still strive to reach us? Who can say?"

Feeling very odd indeed, as if *she* might be the only one who could answer that question for sure, Rose Rita began to read the chapter about Belle Frisson.

As for Lewis, he despaired more and more as the days went past. Surprisingly, the source of his trouble was not teasing. He found that the other kids didn't make fun of him nearly as much as he expected. The talent show was soon forgotten as other topics came up, such as the high-school football games and the approach of Halloween. Oh, every once in a while someone would cluck like a chicken as Lewis walked past, but more people seemed to remember the "Who's on first?" routine that Dave and Tom had done. The boys had come in third, and lots of people thought they should have won the contest.

Lewis's growing concern came from the way his best friend was behaving. Rose Rita's coolness bothered Lewis a lot. He did not have very many friends, and Rose Rita was the one who understood and liked him best. One afternoon as he and his uncle were raking leaves, Lewis talked to Jonathan about her, and his uncle sympathised. "Growing up is a very rough process," Jonathan told him, leaning on his rake. "Your feelings get bruised, and you don't think you can ever make it, but somehow most people do. Give Rose Rita time to live down her embarrassment, and things will be fine."

"I messed everything up," said Lewis sorrowfully, sweeping wet maple leaves into a musty-smelling scarlet-and-yellow pile.

Jonathan patted him on the shoulder. "Accidents happen. Do you know the notion I had when everything started to go wrong? I thought, 'Lewis and Rose Rita could still save the day if they just turn the whole act into a comedy routine.' But I had no way of telling you that."

Lewis piled his batch of leaves on to the large heap that the two of them had made in a corner of the yard. He considered what his uncle had said, and he wondered why he had not had the same idea at the time. It was true—people had laughed more loudly at him and Rose Rita than they had at Tom and Dave, who had been trying to be funny. If only Lewis had come up with some way to make his bumbling seem part of the act, everything might have turned out differently. Only he hadn't, and the talent show had been the worst night of his life.

That Friday Mrs Zimmermann invited everyone down to her cottage on Lyon Lake. It was too late in the year for swimming, but the cottage was a peaceful place, with a nice view and a cosy atmosphere, and Mrs Zimmermann said she hoped Rose Rita would come along. Rose Rita turned her down, though, so the party consisted of just Mrs Zimmermann, Uncle Jonathan, and a subdued Lewis. Mrs Zimmermann outdid herself at making a tasty dinner, with grilled pork chops, fluffy stuffed baked potatoes, tangy cabbage slaw, freshly baked bread, sweet creamy butter, and an enormous apple pie with ice cream for dessert. They ate everything off her purple plates, wiped their lips with purple napkins, and sighed in contentment.

"That was wonderful, Florence," said Jonathan

with a broad smile that shone through his red beard. "I don't think you've ever done better."

"Why, thank you, Weird Beard," returned Mrs Zimmermann. Then she sighed too, and her expression became serious. "I'm only sorry that Rose Rita wouldn't come. I'm worried about her."

Stuffed and happy for the moment, Lewis felt his heart sink. "I am too," he admitted. "She barely talks to me any more."

"Well," said Mrs Zimmermann, sipping a cup of coffee, "Rose Rita is at an age when she hates to be embarrassed. It may take her quite a while to get over it."

Jonathan put his hand on Lewis's shoulder. "Lewis is having a rough time too," he said. "He's going to have to put up with all sorts of corny jokes about his act laying an egg for a long, long time."

Lewis couldn't help grinning. It really helped that neither his uncle nor Mrs Zimmermann played down what had happened, or tried to tiptoe around it. They talked about it right out in the open, just as if Lewis were an adult. He liked that about his uncle. Jonathan Barnavelt had a knack for making Lewis feel comfortable even about horrible things like his failure in the talent show.

"Well, Lewis," said Mrs Zimmermann playfully, "do you plan to give up the stage forever?"

Lewis shrugged and used his fork to toy with a few crumbs of pie crust still on his plate. "I don't know. I think everything would've been all right if I hadn't tried to use that chicken. Learning the tricks was a lot of fun."

"Hmm," said Jonathan. "You know, every year there's a big magicians' meeting over in Colon, where a magic-supply house, Abbot's, is located. Maybe next year we can drive over and you can pick up some tricks—that is, if you want to."

Lewis laid his fork down. "I'll have to think about it. Right now I sort of want to be an astronomer. That way I could work in an observatory at night, when everyone else is asleep, and I could look at planets and stars through a telescope instead of being looked at."

"There's a lot to be said for that too," said Jonathan, chuckling. "And now I think it's only fair if we do the dishes to show our appreciation for this magnificent meal." He took a quarter from his pocket. "We'll flip to see who washes and who wipes."

"Uncle Jonathan," said Lewis, "is that your trick, a two-headed quarter?"

For a second Jonathan looked utterly flummoxed. Then he threw his head back and laughed. "Curses! Foiled again! Your choice, Lewis—wash or wipe?"

They had driven down to Lyon Lake in Bessie, Mrs Zimmermann's green Plymouth, because Mrs Zimmermann said she didn't trust Jonathan Barnavelt's driving or his antique car. They drove back late at night. The oaks and maples grew close to the shoulder of Homer Road, making dark tunnels through which the car whizzed.

Lewis knew the moon was just about full, but the thick, dark clouds covered it completely. Now and then a gusty wind swept whirling dry leaves through the glare of the headlights. Lewis, sitting in the back seat, looked between Mrs Zimmermann and Jonathan to peer out at the road ahead.

They bumped across the railroad tracks and back into New Zebedee. All the stores were dark and locked. Mrs Zimmermann turned on to Mansion Street, and a moment later Lewis glanced at Rose Rita's house. He felt frozen for an instant, and then he yelped.

Mrs Zimmermann stepped hard on the brake, and Bessie screeched to a halt. "What in the name of Heaven?"

"Look!" said Lewis. "Look at Rose Rita's house!"

Jonathan rolled down the passenger window. In a shaky voice he asked, "Is that a dog?"

"No," replied Lewis. The dark shape moving in jerks and starts on Rose Rita's porch was big enough to be a collie or a Labrador, but it was no dog. It had stalky legs, far too many of them.

"It's a shadow," said Mrs Zimmermann uncertainly. "Just the shadow of a tree."

The dark shape ran straight up the wall in unnerving silence.

"No," Jonathan said tensely. "It's no shadow. It's a spider—a spider as big as a steamer trunk!"

Lewis gasped, his heart racing. The creature scrambled up to the roof and then rose into the sky, as if it were climbing an invisible strand of spider-web. "What is it doing here?" he asked nervously.

"I have no idea," said Jonathan, craning his head out and looking into the sky. "Whatever it is, it's gone now. Florence, I think we have to have a council of war about this. That was no real spider. It's a creature of magic—and of evil. And I have the feeling that Rose Rita is in terrible danger."

CHAPTER EIGHT

The next day was a cool, breezy Saturday. Lewis had taken to dropping in at the National Museum of Magic for half an hour every weekend to talk to Mr Hardwick and his poker friends. On this Saturday he did not go but hung around the house, fighting the feeling that something horrible was coming, like a storm building up on the horizon.

Uncle Jonathan and Mrs Zimmermann were deep in conversation in the study. Lewis had told them all about what he had seen, and they were worried. They were so busy that Lewis felt like an intruder. Finally Jonathan kindly told Lewis it might be better if he paid his usual visit to the museum. "Florence and I aren't much company for you right now," explained Jonathan, "and I really think Mr Hardwick appreciates your interest in his museum. It might take your mind off your troubles, anyway."

Lewis wanted to forget his troubles more than anything else. He found his jacket and stepped out into the crisp morning. He walked towards downtown thoughtfully, and when he passed Rose Rita's house, he crossed to the other side of the street and kept looking anxiously at the trees, half expecting to see a horrible grey shape there, ready to drop down and seize him.

Nothing happened, though. He saw nothing in the trees more strange or frightening than dead leaves, a few fat black squirrels, and one or two old, ratty-looking birds' nests. When Lewis got to the museum, he found that Mr Perkins was late, and the other three men were sitting around trying to fool each other with card tricks while they waited for him to arrive. "You never did tell us how your magic show came out," said Mr Hardwick as he shuffled the deck of cards and then made the jacks pop up from the top one by one. Lewis sighed and told the whole ghastly story.

All three of the magicians listened sympathetically. Mr Mussenberger assured Lewis that such accidents were common. "Try dressing up in a floppy clown outfit and doing tricks on five," he said comfortingly in his rumbling voice. "I've had rabbits misbehave and children give away the secrets of my tricks on the air, and once I produced a big, delicious bottle of Twin Oaks milk, took a huge swig, and spat all over the camera lens because it had turned sour!"

"Even Houdini made mistakes," little Johnny Stone said, reaching for the cards. "Once or twice he had to be rescued when his escapes went wrong. He used to tell a story about how he was doing an underwater escape in the winter, and when he got out of the crate he was locked in, he found himself trapped under the ice in the river! He said he had to swim half a mile on his back, breathing the little bit of air sandwiched between the ice and the water. He got back to shore only seconds before he would have frozen."

Lewis could picture only too clearly the dark water and the terrible barrier of ice, and he could almost feel the deadly embrace of the frigid river. "Did that really happen?" asked Lewis in awe.

Mr Stone winked. "It made a good story, anyway," he said. "Did you see Houdini's milk can downstairs?"

Lewis shook his head. Mr Hardwick got to his feet. "Well, there's no time like the present!" he said. They trooped downstairs, and Mr Hardwick showed Lewis the big galvanised milk can, as tall as Lewis. Eight mammoth padlocks held the lid tightly closed. "Imagine climbing into that thing and letting someone lock you in," said Mr Hardwick. "Imagine how dark and tight it would be in there. No light and no air."

Lewis shuddered at the thought. And then something else struck him. Mrs Zimmermann had spoken about finding Rose Rita in the janitor's closet after the talent show. Lewis remembered that Rose Rita was claustrophobic—being in closed-in places made her very scared. Hiding in a closet was a very unlikely thing for Rose Rita to do. "Excuse me?" Lewis asked. Mr Hardwick had stopped talking and was looking at him.

"I can see you were imagining being inside this thing," said the museum owner. "I asked, can you also imagine how in the world Houdini managed to escape when it was locked this way?"

Lewis shook his head. "It looks impossible."

"It can be done," said Mr Stone smugly.

Mr Hardwick agreed, "Oh, of course it can be done. Still, Houdini did it with *style*. He may have been more an escape artist than a magician, but you have to admit, he did everything with style."

Someone tapped on the door, and Mr Hardwick grinned. "That must be the *late* Mr Thomas Perkins," he said, going to the front of the store.

It wasn't Mr Perkins. Lewis was amazed when Mr Hardwick opened the door and Rose Rita stepped inside. She looked as if she hadn't slept very well for days. Dark circles made her eyes look tired and sunken, and her hair was even stringier than usual. She held a green book close to her chest. "Hi," she said quietly as she handed the book to Mr Hardwick. "Thanks for lending this to me."

"You're certainly welcome," replied Mr Hardwick.

Rose Rita had not noticed Lewis. She licked her lips. "I'd like to keep it a little longer, if you don't mind. Uh, do you ever go to that cemetery you were telling us about? The one where Belle Frisson is buried?"

"Now and then," said Mr Hardwick. "Some of my old friends are buried nearby, and my wife and I visit their graves. A surprising number of magicians have chosen to be buried there and over in Colon, you know." He handed the book back to Rose Rita. "Keep this as long as you want."

"Are you going soon?" Rose Rita asked anxiously.

Mr Hardwick thought for a moment. "Hmm. Now that you mention it, I haven't made the trip in a while. Maybe Ellen and I will drive down tomorrow."

"May I go too, please?" asked Rose Rita.

Mr Hardwick said, "Why, sure, if your parents don't mind." He turned and asked, "Lewis, would you like to tag along?"

Lewis could not answer for a moment. Rose Rita's eyes had darted towards him when Mr Hardwick had spoken, and an expression of furious anger had flickered across her face. Then, like a flash of lightning, it was gone, and her face had the worrisome, slack expression Lewis had seen too often lately. He stammered, "S-sure, I guess. I'll have to ask my uncle."

"By all means," said Mr Hardwick. He looked

out the door. "Well, Tom Perkins is parking his old rattletrap across the street, so our poker game can begin at last."

Lewis said goodbye to Mr Hardwick and the others, and he and Rose Rita walked away. Lewis murmured a few words to her, but Rose Rita either grunted or shrugged in response. When they got to her house, she just walked away from Lewis without a word. Lewis had the eerie feeling that somehow the person he had walked from the museum with really wasn't Rose Rita. *She's like a walking corpse*, he thought. The idea made him feel nauseated and weak. If Rose Rita was not living inside her body, then who was? Or, even worse—*what* was?

When he got home, Lewis found Mrs Zimmermann and Uncle Jonathan still sitting in the study. Jonathan was behind the big desk with the green-shaded lamp, an untidy stack of books at his elbow. Mrs Zimmermann sat in one of the big armchairs, busily knitting something that looked like a long purple scarf. She rarely knitted, but sometimes when she had to do a lot of thinking, she dragged out her yarn and her needles and started to work on something that might turn out to be a baggy sweater, a comforter, or a shawl. She always said that whatever turned out surprised her just as much as anybody, since she simply began to knit with no object in mind.

Both Mrs Zimmermann and Uncle Jonathan glanced up as Lewis came in and settled into the other armchair. "You look bewitched, bothered, and bewildered, Lewis," said Mrs Zimmermann as her needles clicked away.

Lewis nodded. "I thought about something a while ago," he said, and told Mrs Zimmermann how odd it was that Rose Rita had chosen to hide in a broom closet.

"I've already mentioned that," replied Mrs Zimmermann. "In fact, Jonathan and I have been talking about how strangely Rose Rita has been acting lately—she isn't quite herself. We've been doing a little research on that—and

on the spider thing we all saw at her house."
Lewis shivered when Mrs Zimmermann said
that. She gave him a strained sort of smile, as
if she were trying to look happier than she
really felt. "Cheer up! Fuzzy Face and I have
been looking through his volumes of mystic
lore, and we think that whatever that grim grey
beastie was, it probably can't hurt Rose Rita."

"It isn't that, exactly," said Lewis with a sigh.
He told them about meeting Rose Rita at the
museum. "She wants to go with Mr Hardwick
to this grave tomorrow," he finished. "And I
don't want to go along." He bit his lower lip.
If he had dared, he would have confessed that
the idea of travelling down to Cristobal scared
the wits out of him. He did not like spooky
cemeteries. Nor did he relish riding twenty miles
into the country in the back seat of a car with
Rose Rita—not when she was acting so odd.

Jonathan Barnavelt exchanged glances with
Mrs Zimmermann. "Haggy Face," he said, "this
opportunity might be the very answer to our
problem. Do you agree?"

Mrs Zimmermann perked up. "I surely do. Enough sitting around and moping and wondering what disaster is going to happen next! I say it's time for action, and I say that Lewis can be a big help."

Jonathan tugged at his red beard. "I think Florence is right, Lewis," he said slowly. "You see, we believe that Rose Rita has somehow come under a magical attack. In order to fight it, we have to know what's behind it—or more to the point, *who's* behind it. So you'll have to be our eyes and ears. I think you should go along on this trip and see what you can get out of Rose Rita."

Lewis sighed helplessly. "She won't even talk to me," he said.

Mrs Zimmermann clicked her tongue irritably as she dropped a stitch. She worked back over it and said, "That's why you'll have to be sort of a secret agent, Lewis. Oh, I know it's not nice to spy on your friends, and ordinarily I'd never suggest such a thing. In this case, though, Jonathan is right. I can practically feel my thumbs pricking, like the witches' thumbs in *Macbeth*. Something wicked is coming our way, and we'll be sunk if we don't learn what we're dealing with. You'll have to be observant, and you'll have to remember every little thing. But it could save Rose Rita."

Lewis pondered that as he watched Mrs Zimmermann's needles busily add another row of stitches to the growing garment. Finally he took a deep breath. "OK," he said at last. "I don't like it, but I'll do it."

And so it was settled. Jonathan and Mrs Zimmermann conferred all afternoon, and dinner was a hurried affair of cold chicken sandwiches and potato chips. Throughout the evening Lewis was restless. He wandered around the house, searching for something he could not name and would not recognise if he saw it.

The old mansion was a great place to live, and Lewis loved it there. Each room had its own fireplace, and every fireplace was made of marble of a different colour. The upstairs rooms were rarely used, and a great variety of junk was stored there, including trunks of Barnavelt stuff that dated from before the Civil War, a wheezy antique parlour organ, and a stereopticon with about five hundred 3D sepia-toned photographs of everything from the Pyramids of Egypt to a tightrope walker poised on a wire high above Niagara Falls. Usually Lewis could spend a rainy day very happily, just exploring and trying out the wonderful things he found.

But that Saturday evening he felt at loose ends. He was too nervous to sit still, and he had nothing to keep him occupied. So he roamed instead. He spent a little while sitting on the back stairs, gazing at the stained-glass window. Jonathan had cast a spell on it, and it changed every time you looked. Sometimes there were strange scenes that might be from another planet—tall smoking volcanoes, weird twisted trees, and inexplicable buildings in the shapes of spheres, cones, and cylinders. Usually there were more earthly subjects—a knight slaying a dragon; shepherds playing lyres, tambouras, and syrinxes while tending their sheep; or four angels dancing the tango.

That evening the stained-glass window showed a road stretching through a landscape of rolling, wooded hills. The sky above the road was a dark purply blue. The hills were a deep, gloomy green, and the road wound between them like a flat grey snake. The picture seemed to pull Lewis in, and he imagined travelling down that mysterious road under the strange and threatening sky. What would lie at the end? He sighed, got up, and went to see if there was something to watch on TV.

Later that night, in bed, Lewis brooded over his sense of coming doom. He was frightened without knowing what frightened him. He felt trapped. He sensed that some evil intelligence was watching him, knowing what he would do and planning to destroy him. The sinister image of that winding road kept returning to his mind, and he kept wondering what terrifying end the road might have. Lewis tried to tell himself not to be such a coward, but that did no good.

Lewis just wasn't the kind of person who could ignore doubt and danger. His chest ached, and he felt terribly alone. A prayer came into his mind.

Lewis felt a little better. He faced an adversity that he couldn't even begin to understand, and he hoped that his plea for help would be answered. At last, still tossing and turning, he fell into a light and troubled sleep.

CHAPTER NINE

Sunday was one of those autumn days with a deep blue sky and the kind of high, wispy, streaky cirrus clouds called mares' tails. Mr Hardwick and his wife, Ellen, a slight, brown-eyed woman who wore a straw sun hat, called for Lewis in their blue-and-white Chevrolet. Rose Rita was already in the back seat, and Lewis joined her. They didn't talk much on the trip to Cristobal; Rose Rita was still distant and quiet. Lewis stared out of the car window instead as they passed farms with old red barns, their roofs bearing advertising signs. Mr Hardwick was a good, careful driver, and they took their time.

Cristobal was hardly a town at all. New Zebedee was pretty small, but Cristobal was just a crossroads with a feed store, a general store, and a petrol station. Maybe because New Zebedee had once been in the running to be named the capital city of Michigan, its houses tended to be old and rather elegant, Victorian affairs with towers, gingerbread decorations, and gabled roofs. The houses in Cristobal were more modest, little white frame buildings with small yards.

Mr Hardwick drove through Cristobal. They passed a big brick church with a cemetery nearby, but they didn't stop. Then they were out in the country again, and Mr Hardwick turned down a winding side road. After a mile or so the road simply ended at another cemetery, this one small and square. A freshly painted old white wooden fence encircled the graveyard. Mr Hardwick stopped the car, and everyone got out. Lewis looked around. The cemetery had no trees at all. Many of the tombstones were old and granite. They were not fancy. Instead of being carved into angels, urns, and monuments, these stones were simple slabs with rounded tops, weathered and grey and splotched with green circles of lichen. One marker stood out.

Mr Hardwick had taken a basket out of the Chevrolet's trunk. It contained two pairs of gardening gloves, grass clippers, and a few other tools. "Ellen and I will tidy up some of the graves," he said. "Both of you can wander around if you like. Rose Rita, that big monument in the middle is Belle Frisson's grave. It's pretty strange. You might want to have a look."

The grass was a little high in the cemetery. Lewis thought that people probably came out occasionally to keep things neat. Many of the graves had flowers on them, some bright and fresh, others brown and withered. He and Rose Rita walked slowly towards the centre of the cemetery, the gravel crunching under their feet. One of Lewis's superstitions was that something bad would happen to him if he stepped on a grave, so he trod carefully.

"Sure is big," said Lewis as he and Rose Rita stopped in front of the mysterious tombstone. The whole monument rested on a square base ten feet long on each side. On top of the base was a stone cube five feet on each facet, then a many-sided pillar that rose for about ten feet, and finally at the summit a grey ball at least three feet in diameter. For some reason it had several faint chalk marks on it. Everything, from the base to the ball, was a gloomy-looking dark grey granite. The cube that supported both the pillar and the ball had words engraved on it:

BELLE FRISSON

(Born Elizabeth Proctor)

1822-1878

She waits to live again

Lewis could hear the *click-click* of grass clippers behind him. He looked up from the inscription.

The pillar on top of the cube wasn't very thick, maybe two feet or so in diameter. It had marks carved deeply into it, curlicues and lines, but they were not letters. Lewis looked at the ball again. Something about it made him feel very apprehensive.

Rose Rita was slowly walking around the grave, studying the pillar intently. Lewis had had enough. He turned and hurried back down the gravel path to the Hardwicks, who were trimming the grass around a headstone inscribed with the name "Frederick Jeremy McCandles: The Great Candelini."

"Weird monument, isn't it?" Mr Hardwick asked Lewis. The museum owner patted his forehead with a handkerchief. "Belle Frisson's, I mean. She died here, you know."

Lewis shook his head.

"Tell him the story," Mrs Hardwick urged. "Halloween's coming soon! It's a good time to hear it."

"Well," said Mr Hardwick, clipping more grass, "back in 1878 Belle Frisson was touring the country, doing her communicating-with-the-dead act. She had made an appearance in Detroit and was heading west by train. Just outside Cristobal the train jumped the tracks. Quite a few people were hurt."

"It was a famous accident," Mrs Hardwick added. "It happened in the middle of October on a clear, dry night, and no one ever discovered the cause."

Mr Hardwick agreed. "It was very puzzling. Many injuries, as I said, but only Belle Frisson's were serious. There used to be a farm right here, owned by a doctor. He and his wife took Belle Frisson in to treat her injuries. She regained consciousness, but she knew she wasn't going to make it. So on her deathbed she did something very eccentric. She arranged to buy the doctor's farm from him."

"Was she rich?" asked Lewis.

"Rich enough," replied Mr Hardwick. "She spent nearly a week sketching out her tombstone, ordering it to be made exactly the way she drew it. Then strange people came to the farm—

people the doctor had certainly not telegraphed, people whom Belle Frisson couldn't possibly have contacted in any normal way. She saw them one at a time and gave them some kind of orders. She also told the doctor that she was going to be buried in the front yard of the farm. And she wrote out her will. She also created a very peculiar scroll that I have in the museum. She died on Halloween night, 1878. The next day the doctor and his wife moved away. Those outsiders came—stonemasons, carpenters, an undertaker, I don't know what—and they spent a month burying Belle and putting up that monument. Then they dismantled the house and went away."

"They left just the one grave," said Mrs Hardwick. "Over the years, that changed. Belle Frisson's will said that anyone who couldn't afford a burial anywhere else could have a plot for free. Any magician could also be buried in this cemetery."

Mr Hardwick continued. "About six or seven conjurors have taken her up on the offer." He patted the grave that he was working on. "Freddy, here, better known as the Great Candelini, is one of them. I knew him. He passed away, at the ripe old age of eighty-seven, and he asked to be buried here. He had a great act that used lighted candles. You would have liked him, Lewis."

Lewis nodded. "Why are there chalk marks on the ball on top of Belle Frisson's monument?" he asked.

Mr Hardwick put the clippers back in the basket and got up. "That's another peculiar thing. The ball rotates. It moves very slowly. It makes one complete revolution about every six weeks. Nobody can tell how it works though one science teacher told me it probably has to do with the way the granite expands when the weather is warm and contracts when it cools off again."

"People put chalk marks on the ball to prove that it moves," explained Mrs Hardwick. "And sure enough it does."

The two of them began to clean up another

grave, and Lewis walked back towards Belle Frisson's monument. He could not shake a creepy sensation that something was very wrong, and he was worried about Rose Rita. He stopped dead in his tracks when he saw her, standing on the far side of the monument. She had her arms spread out, her palms turned towards the sky, and her head thrown back. The sunlight glinted on her glasses. She seemed to be staring at the ball on top of the monument.

"Hi," he said, coming up to her. She did not answer. "Pretty strange tombstone."

Rose Rita glared at him. "You don't know anything about it," she snapped.

Lewis raised his eyebrows. "What? What's eating you? I just said—"

"Forget it."

Lewis went on, "Mr Hardwick says the ball up there rotates. It turns all by itself. That's why people have put chalk marks on it. Weird, huh?"

"Where movement is, there is life also," replied Rose Rita in a strange, hoarse voice.

"Blood is the life, and as from one it may be taken, to another it shall be given."

"What are you talking about?" asked Lewis.

Rose Rita shook her head. "Nothing."

The day began to feel very cold to Lewis, though the sun still shone through the clouds. The *snip-snip* of the garden shears, the rustle of a breeze through the grass, were the only sounds. "What do you suppose those marks are?" asked Lewis, trying to fill in the silence. He pointed to the curves and swirls carved into the granite shaft.

"A mystery," replied Rose Rita in that same harsh, dreamy voice. "One that may be wrapped up or unwrapped in time. One whose answer may be fetched from afar."

Something tickled Lewis's neck. He slapped at it, thinking it was a bug. He felt something stringy and looked at his fingers. A thin strand of cobweb connected them. Grimacing in revulsion, he stooped and scrubbed his hand on the grass. Then he felt another light touch on his face, and another. Crying out in alarm,

Lewis began to flail around in the air. It was full of wispy, floating strands of cobweb—and at the end of each strand was a tiny, almost invisible, grey spider. Lewis hated spiders. He grabbed Rose Rita's arm. "Let's get out of here!" he said, dragging her down the path.

The floating baby spiders vanished as soon as they were a few steps away from the Frisson grave. Lewis told the Hardwicks about them, and they thought the baby spiders were probably just migrating. "I've heard of them doing that," said Mr Hardwick. "Thought they did it in the spring, though."

Rose Rita didn't say anything, and she said very little on the way back to New Zebedee. Lewis watched her, tried to remember her exact words, and brooded.

That evening he told Uncle Jonathan and Mrs Zimmermann about everything that he remembered. They listened gravely, and when he finished, they exchanged long looks. "Does this tomb with its revolving ball sound familiar to you, Jonathan?" asked Mrs Zimmermann.

"It sounds like something out of the Egyptian Book of the Dead," responded Jonathan. "What about the spiders? Wasn't there something about spiders in Egyptian mythology?"

Mrs Zimmermann touched a finger to her chin. "Hmm. I don't remember anything especially about spiders. Of course, the Egyptians placed great importance in the scarab, which is a type of beetle, but spiders aren't even insects, so that wouldn't apply. I'm coming up blank. I can remember the myth of Arachne, whom the gods turned into a spider, and I can recall the African folk tales about Anansi, the trickster spider, but that's all."

"It's a mystery," pronounced Jonathan.

"One whose answer may be fetched from afar," said Lewis solemnly. Both Uncle Jonathan and Mrs Zimmermann stared at him as though he had suddenly sprouted an extra head. "What is it?" he asked, a little alarmed.

"That was a mighty odd thing to say," replied

Jonathan. "One whose answer may be fetched from afar? What is that supposed to mean?"

"I don't know," confessed Lewis. "It's something Rose Rita said."

"She used those exact words?" asked Jonathan, his voice troubled.

"Yes, I'm pretty sure," Lewis said. "If not those words, almost the same ones."

Jonathan took a pipe cleaner—he still carried them around, though he never smoked any more—from his vest and twisted it into the shape of a spring. He pressed the ends together until the pipe cleaner slipped out of his fingers and leaped away. Then he said tightly, "Florence, I may be a fussbudget and a gloomy Gus, but that has a bad sound to me. You know all about fetches, of course."

"Ye-s-s," she said. "Still, it could be a coincidence."

"What are fetches?" asked Lewis.

Jonathan looked sombrely at Mrs Zimmermann. "You explain them, Haggy. You're the professional here."

"Well, Lewis," Mrs Zimmermann began, "a fetch is a kind of apparition or spirit. In England and Ireland fetches take the form of a person. In fact they are identical to the person they apply to. That kind of fetch is what the Germans call a *Doppelganger,* which more or less means 'walking double.' Anyway, usually a friend or family member sees the fetch of a victim—"

"V-victim?" stammered Lewis. Now he knew he wasn't going to like learning about fetches.

Jonathan nodded. "Sometimes even the victim himself or herself sees the fetch. Usually other people mistake it for the victim."

"That's a human kind of fetch," said Mrs Zimmermann. "In other countries and other time periods, though, people believed in other kinds. They might be animals, or birds, or insects."

"Or s-spiders?" guessed Lewis.

"Yes, or spiders," answered Mrs Zimmermann. "All fetches, whether animal or bird or creepy-crawlies, have one job to do, and that is how they get their name. They are sent forth to fetch the soul of a doomed person."

"And the person dies?" asked Lewis in a small voice.

Softly, Uncle Jonathan replied, "That's right, Lewis. The person dies."

Lewis didn't say anything. He could only think of his friend, Rose Rita, and of the terrible spider they had seen outside her house. Was it truly a fetch? Was Rose Rita doomed to die?

CHAPTER TEN

That Sunday afternoon Rose Rita was getting ready to leave the house. Her mother called, "Where are you going, dear?"

Rose Rita was wearing jeans, a bulky jacket, and a purple knit cap that Mrs Zimmermann had made for her. She yelled back, "Lewis and I are going to study for a big test. I probably won't be back until late."

"Don't be too late," Mrs Pottinger called.

Rose Rita dashed outside. She had several things stuffed inside her jacket: the scroll, the book, a torch, and a couple of sandwiches wrapped in waxed paper. In a way she felt very guilty about what she was going to do. Rose Rita liked to tell outrageous stories, but she almost never lied to her parents. She climbed on to her bike and rode downtown, pumping away like a machine. She headed west, past the fountain and the National House Hotel, and then out into the countryside.

She rode for maybe three or four miles before finally climbing off her bike. She looked around. Just north of the highway was a cornfield, with the brown, dry cornstalks still standing. It had a three-rail fence around it, but that was no problem. Rose Rita climbed the fence, then wrestled her bike through. It was easy to hide the bike in the corn. Rose Rita headed back down to the highway and began to hitchhike.

Six cars zoomed past without even slowing. Then a rusty red Ford pickup came sputtering along, slowed, and pulled over. A plump woman opened the passenger door. "Need a ride, dearie?" she asked in a cheerful voice. "Climb in!"

Rose Rita did. "Thank you," she said.

The woman banged the truck into gear. "That's all right, dearie. My name's Susanna Seidler. What's yours?"

"Rowena Potter," declared Rose Rita, who had already made up the fake name.

"Well, Rowena Potter, where are you bound?"

"I'm trying to get back to Cristobal," said Rose Rita.

Mrs Seidler had the broad, red face of a farmer, and she wore a red-and-black checked flannel shirt and overalls with a big red bandanna tied around her neck. Her hair was short, straight, and copper red. She gave Rose Rita a surprised look from cornflower-blue eyes. "My stars, Rowena, that's quite a long way. How'd you get clear over to New Zebedee?"

Rose Rita stared ahead at the highway. "Well, that's a long story," she said slowly, her mind working furiously. "My uncle had to come into

New Zebedee yesterday to see the doctor. He asked me if I'd ride along with him, so I did. But the doctor decided he had to have his appendix out right then, so he stuck my uncle in the hospital. It was so sudden that nobody thought about me. Anyway, today my uncle asked me if I could get back home to feed his chickens and pigs and let my mum and dad know he's all right."

"You could've just phoned," said Mrs Seidler.

"We don't have a phone," replied Rose Rita. "Both of my parents are deaf."

"My stars!" cried Mrs Seidler. "You certainly have a rough time of it! Why didn't you ask the doctor for help?"

"He's not in New Zebedee any more," said Rose Rita. "As soon as he operated on my uncle, he went off for a week-long fishing trip on the Upper Peninsula."

"I never heard of such a thing!" exclaimed Mrs Seidler indignantly. "Well, Rowena, just you relax. I'll take you right to your front door, because I'm passing through Cristobal. My husband and I have a farm about ten miles past there, so it's no trouble."

Rose Rita bit her lip in consternation. Sometimes her stories were *too* good. She didn't say much else about her family but instead asked Mrs Seidler about hers. Mrs Seidler loved to talk about her children, and as the miles rolled past, Rose Rita heard all about Hiram and Ernst and Clara and Velma, the baby, whom everyone called "Snookums." They drove through Cristobal just before sunset. Rose Rita began to feel anxious. Then she saw a farmhouse on the left. "That's my house," she said hurriedly, stopping Mrs Seidler in the middle of a story about how Snookums had painted the kitchen walls with ketchup.

"I'll drive up and say howdy," said Mrs Seidler, slowing the truck.

"No, that's all right," replied Rose Rita. "They're probably at church anyhow. Thanks for the ride." She insisted until Mrs Seidler just pulled over and let her out of the truck. Rose Rita stood and waved until the rusty old Ford had driven away out of sight. Then she began to walk. The turnoff road to the cemetery was not far past the farmhouse.

Once she got on to the turnoff road, it was a long way, and Rose Rita got hotter and hotter. The sun sank low, and her shadow stretched out long and dark. At last she stood before the strange monument. Squinting up at it, Rose Rita thought the chalk marks had moved a little. The mysterious ball on top of the monument had revolved half an inch or so in the few hours since she had been here. The rugged, pitted grey globe was halfway in ruddy sunlight and halfway in deep shadow. Rose Rita reached inside her jacket and pulled out the scroll. She took it out of its embroidered wrapper and began to unroll it. "Now what do I do?" she muttered aloud.

The answer was startling. Rose Rita squeaked out in surprise as she felt a tug. The scroll seemed to have come to life. It yanked and jerked in her grasp, trying to tear itself free. Holding it was like holding a piece of iron near a very strong magnet. The scroll wanted to leap out of her hands and fly towards the monument. Rose Rita let go.

Whoosh! The scroll unwound! It stretched out to more than twelve feet. It snaked through the air, rippling and fluttering. One end of it caught at the very base of the many-sided pillar, and the other began to fly around and around the shaft. The scroll stretched out, longer and longer, as it wrapped itself around the pillar in a spiral. About an inch of the stone showed between the bands of the scroll. With a final slap the free end of the scroll plastered itself just beneath the sphere. The sun set at that moment, leaving Rose Rita in the sudden chill of twilight.

There was still enough light to see. Rose Rita walked around the pillar, looking up. She gasped. The marks along the edges of the scroll had lined up with those carved into the stone. Together, they made up letters. Rose Rita began to speak them, her heart bursting with terror. Some spell was at work. She could not stop reading the words aloud:

IN THE NAME OF NEITII,
IN THE NAME OF ANUBIS,
IN THE NAME OF OSIRIS, HEAR!

Rose Rita's vision became blurry, though the letters of the chant burned bright and clear. Slowly she walked around the stone shaft in a counterclockwise direction, reading strange, ancient-Egyptian-sounding words in a voice edged with grief and fear.

The air around her seemed to shimmer. The sandwiches and the torch fell from her jacket, but she did not notice. When she tried to stop walking, something drew her on. She had the weird feeling that hundreds of tiny ropes had been tied to her arms and legs, and they dragged her along like a living puppet. She screamed out the last words of the chant, "UR-NIPISHTIM! HORLA! THUT-IM-SHOLA!" Then she stood reeling and exhausted.

Silence dropped around her. Rose Rita had no sense that any time had passed, but overhead, stars shone in a dark sky, and a gibbous moon was rising in the east. In its light everything looked different. The tombstones were like snaggly teeth jutting from ancient gums. The tomb before her resembled a tall, standing figure glaring down at her. The sphere on the top began to spin faster and faster. Sparks began to fly. The sound grew sharper, until Rose Rita fell to her knees and clamped her hands over her ears.

Then, with a rumble that made the ground tremble, the whole monument—cube, shaft, and sphere—shifted, pivoting to the left. The moving cube uncovered a dark, square opening beneath it. Again feeling as if she were being pulled by strings, Rose Rita jerked to her feet and lurched forwards on to stairs carved from stone. They led down into the earth.

"No!" she cried, but it was no use. She hated closed-in spaces, and the opening was more frightening than anything she had known. She tried to scream, but something soft and clinging, something like yards and yards of cobweb, closed her mouth, reducing her to terrified squeaks.

And then she stepped down into the darkness. Overhead, the monument shuddered as it slid back into place. The last rays of light died.

Rose Rita was trapped inside the tomb.

CHAPTER ELEVEN

Lewis was in bed reading when he heard the phone ring. The Westclox alarm clock beside his bed said the time was nine forty-four. Curious, Lewis got out of bed and padded downstairs barefoot to find out who was calling so late.

His uncle stood in the front hall, speaking into the receiver: "No, she hasn't . . . Yes, that's what I'd do . . . I wouldn't worry just yet. I tell you what, Mrs Pottinger, I'll call Mrs Zimmermann. She may have an idea or two . . .

I understand. Certainly . . . Yes, you do that. Goodbye." Jonathan hung up the phone and turned to Lewis, looking very upset. "That was Louise Pottinger. She said Rose Rita came over here around four o'clock to study for a test with you. She didn't, did she?"

Lewis felt cold. "No," he uttered. "I haven't seen her since about two thirty, when the Hardwicks dropped her off at her house. What's happened?"

"She's disappeared," said Jonathan gravely. "Go get dressed, Lewis. I'm going to call Florence. This doesn't sound very good at all."

Lewis hurried back upstairs and got into a fresh pair of corduroy trousers, a shirt, socks, and trainers. By the time he got down to the study, Mrs Zimmermann was already there. "I was afraid something like this might happen," she was saying. She looked up as he came in and gave him a sad kind of smile. "Hello, Lewis! I was just telling your uncle that Rose Rita may be in real trouble."

"I bet it has something to do with that Belle

Frisson," said Lewis. "Rose Rita acted really weird at the cemetery. It was like the monument fascinated her."

"Jonathan and I have checked all our books on magic," Mrs Zimmermann said. "Belle Frisson, whoever she was, doesn't show up in any of them. If she was a real sorceress, she was not one who associated with any other true magicians."

"To tell you the truth," revealed Jonathan, "both Florence and I think that Belle Frisson was just a stage magician—a conjuror, like your friends at the magic museum. I found a mention or two of her name in books on spiritualism and mediums, but that was all. I figured she was like the 'trance mediums' whom Houdini used to expose. He was sort of a detective, you know, specialising in unmasking fakes who claimed to have real powers."

"I didn't know that," replied Lewis.

"Well, be that as it may," said Mrs Zimmermann firmly, "it doesn't help us with our problem. Louise Pottinger is asking the police to find Rose Rita, but if magic is tied up in this, they won't be able to help. It seems to be sorcery of a special kind too—Egyptian magic. If only Dr Walsh were in town, we could consult him."

Dr David Walsh was a great local celebrity. He was an archaeologist who specialised in the history and lore of ancient Egypt, and he had been on many expeditions. In fact, at that moment he was away, excavating a tomb somewhere on the banks of the River Nile in Egypt.

Lewis said, "His son, Chris, goes to the elementary school. I know him."

"That might help," said Jonathan. "Lewis, tomorrow I'd like you to ask Chris if we might take a look at some of his father's books. Dr Walsh has a huge collection dealing with Egypt, and maybe something will be of help."

"Tomorrow? Can't we do anything tonight?" Lewis pleaded.

"Like what?" asked Mrs Zimmermann. "Lewis, we all like Rose Rita a great deal, and we'd do anything to help her. When you're up against the unknown, though, it doesn't do good to go charging in. You have to arm yourself so that you can fight if necessary. Besides, Rose Rita will be all right, at least for a while. Jonathan and I have learned something about fetches. If one has summoned Rose Rita away, that's all it can do for the time being. She will be safe until the next phase of the moon."

"When is that?" asked Lewis, dreading to hear.

"Friday night," said Jonathan. "That's when the moon goes into its last quarter."

"The night before Halloween," whispered Lewis.

"Yes," replied Jonathan in a solemn voice. "The night before Halloween."

If Jonathan and Mrs Zimmermann had guessed right, that meant they had only five days to rescue Rose Rita. Lewis hoped it would be enough.

The next day, school dragged on forever. Rose Rita was absent, and everyone knew she was missing. Many people thought she had run away, and others thought she might have been kidnapped. Some of the kids in Lewis's classes asked him about Rose Rita, but he didn't want to speak about her.

After school Lewis headed over to the Walshs' house. They lived on Michigan Street, several blocks west of High Street. As he walked along, Lewis had the uncanny sense that he was being watched. He turned and looked behind him, but he saw no one. Then he stuck his hands deeper into his jacket pockets, hunched his shoulders, and crunched over dry leaves. He turned a corner suddenly and jumped behind a tree. He waited there, holding his breath.

Half a minute later a hurrying figure came around the corner. Lewis let his breath out and relaxed. He stepped out from behind the tree. "Hey, Chad," he said. "Are you following me?"

Chad Britton, a blond, brown-eyed kid wearing a tan trench coat buttoned up tight, stopped and grinned. "Well, I was," he said ruefully. "I'm practising."

Lewis sighed. Chad wanted to be a detective when he grew up, and he liked to practise by following people around. He was getting pretty good at it. Sometimes he gave older people the heebie-jeebies when they realised he had been silently observing them for an hour or more. "Well, stop it," said Lewis. "I'm not doing anything."

"But you're one of Rose Rita Pottinger's friends," replied Chad reasonably. "Everyone says she's been kidnapped and crooks are holding her for ransom. That's why I was following you."

"*I* wouldn't kidnap Rose Rita," said Lewis angrily.

"I know you wouldn't. But your uncle is rich, so I figured they might kidnap you too and ask him for a lot of ransom money. Then I could get the crooks' licence plate and report it to the police." Chad smiled as if that were the most logical thing in the world.

"I don't think it's going to be that easy," said Lewis. "Anyway, I'm busy right now. Tomorrow I'll tell you everything I know about the case, OK?"

"Great!" Chad consented. "Keep me posted!"

Shaking his head, Lewis walked on to the Walsh house. Chris Walsh, a ten-year-old boy with short, brown hair, was standing in front of the big stone house tossing a football up and catching it. He grinned when he saw Lewis and threw the ball to him. Lewis flinched, missed the ball, and picked it up. Laughing, Chris said, "Hi, Lewis."

"Hi, yourself," Lewis replied, tossing him the football. Chris caught it expertly. "Want to play?" Chris asked.

"I can't right now," Lewis said. "Is your mum home?"

Chris said, "Yes," and Lewis explained what he needed. "My uncle is interested in Egypt," he finished, "and he'd like to borrow a book or two. Especially books on Egyptian magic."

"Oh, sure," said Chris right away. "Dad has lots of those. Come on in."

The house was big, with high ceilings, wainscotted walls, and many Egyptian artefacts. There were urns and statuettes, and on the walls were pieces of ancient bronze armour, funeral masks, and framed sheets of papyrus covered with hieroglyphs. Chris's mother said that Lewis could borrow as many books as he wanted, so they went to the study. Chris walked over to a bookcase and said, "Here's some of the real stuff. This is *The Book of Going Forth by Day*, which most people call the Book of the Dead. And this one is about animal magic. Here's another one . . ."

By the time they had finished, Lewis had a stack of six books, two of them large and heavy. He thanked Chris and his mother and headed back across town. Before he had got even halfway home, Chad Britton started to shadow him again. Lewis ignored him and hurried on to High Street.

Mrs Zimmermann returned, and she and Jonathan pored over the books, taking time only for another hurried dinner of sandwiches.

At last Mrs Zimmermann looked up from her book. "Here's something," she said. "Listen to this." She cleared her throat and began to read:

In pre-dynastic times the curious cult of Neith began in ancient Sais. The followers of the goddess Neith were caught up in the study of the mysteries of life and death. Neith was the Weaver of the World, the terrible Opener of the Way between life and death, and her representative creature, the spider, was a symbolic connection between the two states, with her web the bridge between the here and now and the hereafter. Some worshippers believed that the web of the Great Spider, like the skein of Ariadne, could thread the maze between this world and the dark world of death. They judged that, by following the strand backwards, it might be possible for a departed soul to return to life.

Such a passage would be costly, however. To begin, it would demand the spilling of blood and the creation of the spectral Death Spider. At the termination of the process a human sacrifice would have to be made, blood for blood and life for life. Only by sending a victim into death could the soul anxious to return be granted a passage back to life.

Jonathan Barnavelt whistled. "That sounds pretty ominous. Is there more?"

Mrs Zimmermann read silently for several minutes. Then she looked up. "Yes. This Death Spider is a creature half spirit, half real—a kind of spectre. Just as we guessed, it behaves like a fetch, and its power is tied to the phases of the moon. Rose Rita will be safe until the turning of the moon—or at least she won't be sacrificed until then. That doesn't give us much time. But there's more, I'm afraid."

In a harsh voice, Jonathan said, "Let's have it."

"The spider has magical powers," Mrs Zimmermann said slowly. "Physically, it is very weak, but it can create illusions, it can mislead and trick us, and if it bites us, it could very well kill us. We'll have to be on our guard."

"When do we go?" asked Lewis.

Jonathan shook his head. "Lewis, I can't ask you to help in this. It's too dangerous." In a kindly voice, he added, "It might be very frightening."

Lewis said quietly, "I know. I'm terrified already. Only, Rose Rita is my friend. Back when that evil spirit nearly lured me into a well, she showed up to help. She needs me now."

Mrs Zimmermann agreed briskly. "I think Lewis is right, Jonathan. The powers of evil have dreadful tricks up their sleeves, but they don't always count on simple things that might foul them up. One of the simplest and most powerful is friendship. All for one and one for all, I say."

Jonathan Barnavelt tugged at his red beard. "All for one and one for all it is, then," he said.

"Lewis, go get our torches. Florence, maybe you'd better go home and pick up some especially powerful amulets and talismans. If we're going up against this Death Spider, we'll need every bit of help we can get!"

CHAPTER TWELVE

When Rose Rita stepped into the dark hollow of the tomb, she had a moment of pure panic. She had the feeling that the walls were slowly coming together to crush her. The air turned dead and stale, and it was hard to breathe. Her lungs throbbed, and her heart felt squeezed, as if it were about to burst in her chest. The world began to spin around and around, and she staggered, dazed and dizzy.

Then some force pulled her along. The passageway slanted downwards, like a ramp, and then became a kind of tunnel. To her astonishment, Rose Rita could see. No light from the surface could come through the earth and stone around her, but some strange, dim, greenish illumination let her glimpse walls made of crumbling grey tiles, with roots and earth bulging through here and there. The floor underfoot was unpleasantly soft and spongy, and things squelched under her feet, popping in a horrible liquid way. A bad smell filled her nostrils, earthy, damp, and mouldy, reminding her of mildew, of rot and decay. Ahead of her the passage turned, but the muted green light—it was almost like a faintly glowing haze in the air—let her see only dimly. Rose Rita took step after unwilling step, her path turning left, then right, then left again, and always leading down, down, down.

She walked for what seemed like hours. At last the light began to grow stronger. She had the sense of tons of earth above her, cutting her off from the surface and from life. As the light increased, Rose Rita could see dark, slimy streaks where water had oozed down the tiled walls of the passage. She could see, too, that she was walking on a leathery carpet of fungi—bloated, pale toadstools that were an ugly, fleshy colour and that released a sickening stench when she stepped on them and made them pop.

The passageway widened to at least ten feet and led to an arch. A filmy curtain swayed softly and gently in the air. As she came closer, Rose Rita held her breath. The swagging silk was not a curtain. It was an enormous spider-web. Small bones were stuck throughout, perhaps the bones of bats, rats, or snakes that had come down here. The arch was far above her head, but even so, Rose Rita cringed as she passed under it.

She stepped out into a strange, round room. The arched ceiling soared high overhead, its hollow centre lost in darkness. In the middle of the room was a round marble platform, with steps leading up to it from all sides. A tall white pillar was centred on the platform, and a broad, white marble bowl rested on top of it. In this marble cauldron something burned with a slow, green flame. Glowing green smoke rose, spread lazily, and drifted through the air. The flame and the vapour were the sources of the bizarre dim light. "Come!"

Rose Rita gasped. She could not tell if the voice was in her head or if the word had been spoken aloud. The deadly force that gripped her made her move around the edge of the platform. Against the wall on the far side stood two thrones. They gleamed dully, like gold. Both thrones had high backs, and crowning each was an odd bust. It looked like a creature with a man's shoulders but the head of some fox-faced animal with enormous ears. Rose Rita had seen pictures of such a being in books. It was Anubis, an ancient Egyptian god, she thought as she moved slowly forwards. She vaguely recalled that Anubis guarded the passageway from life to death . . .

"Welcome," said the harsh, whispering voice, and Rose Rita jerked her attention back to the two thrones. The one on the right was empty.

A spectral figure, as erect and proud as a queen, sat in the other.

"Stop."

Rose Rita halted. She stared at the seated figure. From this close she could tell the figure was a woman, slim and regal looking. She wore a flowing white robe. Her arms rested on the arms of the throne, each hand on top of a golden globe. The skin on her hands and fingers looked unhealthy, grey and strangely pebbly in texture. Her face was in shadow, and she remained motionless. "Welcome."

Rose Rita swayed and collapsed to her hands and knees. She felt as though a string had been supporting her and had suddenly been cut. She shuddered as her hands touched the squelchy toadstools, plunging down into their cold slime up to her wrists. Crying out, she scrambled backwards, up on to the steps of the platform. "Who—who are you?" Rose Rita screamed.

Laughter came from the figure—hissing, cold laughter. "You know who I am."

Rose Rita's teeth chattered. Her hands felt

cold. She frantically scrubbed them against her jeans legs, trying to remove the awful fluids of the fungi. The air in the cavernous room was freezing, and she could not stop shaking. "Belle Frisson," said Rose Rita in a low growl. "What are you doing to me?"

"Nothing that you have not cheerfully done to yourself," the voice said callously. "Did you not want revenge? Did you not hate those who mocked you? Did you not wish to loose the Death Spider?"

"N-no," stammered Rose Rita. "Maybe I daydreamed—"

"You will have all eternity to dream now," responded the whispery voice. "This, though, I promise you: when I go forth once more into the waking world, my first task will be to destroy those who mistreated you. You may reflect on that as you rest here forever."

Rose Rita reeled. Visions flashed before her eyes. Visions of the other girls in her class screaming in terror. Visions of the whole school flaring into flame, burning though it was made of stone. Visions of New Zebedee itself laid waste, everything broken, shattered, ruined, with spiders creeping over the rubble. Then it all cleared away. "You can't do that!" shouted Rose Rita, angry and terrified at the same time.

"I have waited too long," replied the still figure. "I will live again, oh, I will live! But first I will destroy!"

"W-why?" wailed Rose Rita.

The voice was cruel, remorseless. "When I lived the life of flesh, I spoke to spirits! Had I had time to refine my studies, I might have become most powerful, the ruler of the universe—but I had to perform for fools to earn my bread. Ancient spirits taught me, nurtured me, showed me a way of perhaps holding off death. I—arranged for certain procedures to be done in the event of my death. My apparent death. For the vessel was broken, yet the spirit continued."

"I don't understand," complained Rose Rita. Her arms and legs were beginning to feel numb from the terrible cold.

"Of course not!" The voice was a whiplash that made Rose Rita flinch. "Foolish girl, how could you understand the thread of the spider? How could you appreciate how it may hold and bind a spirit, saving it from the final journey to the realms of the dead? I understood! I prepared! And now here you are, to take my place, that I may again don flesh and walk forth among the living! Do you know how a spider lives? How she traps prey and then drinks the blood from it? A small fly's life might last a few weeks, but trapped and wrapped by a spider, the fly lives many times that span! So shall you live, here, seated on the Throne of Anubis, and your long, long life shall be mine, for I am as the spider, drinking from your strength and life!"

Something chittered behind Rose Rita. She turned, dreading what she might see.

A huge spider, the size of a horse, had climbed up on to the platform behind her. Its enormous dark-grey body pulsed in a hideous way. Its five bulging black eyes glittered in the unearthly light.

Its jaws quivered and clenched, revealing sharp, scarlet-tipped fangs that glistened with venom. The hairy beast moved towards Rose Rita.

Rose Rita backed away, her heart thundering. The spider crept forwards. Rose Rita's lungs were paralysed. She wanted to scream, but she could not. She took another step back, off the platform, and another—

And a bony hand seized her arm!

Gasping, Rose Rita turned to fight.

The creature on the throne held her arm in her deadly grip. Rose Rita stared at the woman and felt as if she were going insane.

A skeleton was inside the white linen robe—a skeleton with hollow eye sockets and a fierce grin. The skeleton had a horrible kind of flesh on its bones—for over every inch of its face, swarming and spinning, crawled millions and millions of tiny spiders, their eyes shimmering, their busy legs thrashing.

The skeleton's grinning mouth moved, and the whispery voice said, "They weave me new flesh to wear. It will do. It will do."

And then Rose Rita felt the firm clutch of two of the huge spider's legs, one on each of her shoulders. Everything went dark. She fainted dead away.

CHAPTER THIRTEEN

"Turn here," said Lewis. Mrs Zimmermann turned the wheel, and Bessie rolled off the highway and on to the lane leading out to the cemetery.

Jonathan Barnavelt, sitting in the back seat, said, "This is certainly a deserted patch of ground."

Mrs Zimmermann sniffed. "When villains and evil-doers want to set up housekeeping, they don't march right into the centre of town, Weird Beard. They like to keep their nefarious activity under the cover of darkness and loneliness."

Lewis stared straight ahead. The headlights made a wavering tunnel of light in the night. Finally the lane widened, and Lewis could see the jutting, rounded forms of headstones. "The big one in the middle is Belle Frisson's grave," whispered Lewis. Though he was willing to do anything to help Rose Rita, he had to face the fact that he was sick with anxiety.

The car bounced to a stop, and Mrs Zimmermann turned the key in the ignition. "Well," she said, "here we are. I suppose there's no sense putting things off. Have you got the torches, Jonathan?"

"Right here." He handed two long chrome-plated torches forwards, and he kept another for himself. They were powerful six-cell lights, and they could throw a beam a long way. Before they had left New Zebedee, Jonathan had put new D-cell batteries into all three torches. When Lewis switched his on, the car flooded with bright white light.

"Let's go," said Mrs Zimmermann, opening her door. They all got out.

The countryside was quiet. A light wind ruffled the dry leaves clinging to the trees. A solitary cricket chirped, its song slow, sad, and soft. Four or five silvery clouds drifted across the sky, faintly lit by starlight. The moon was low in the sky. Lewis stood for a few seconds, breathing in great lungfuls of the crisp, cool October air. His uncle put a hand on his shoulder, making Lewis jump a mile.

"Sorry, Lewis," said Jonathan.

"That's OK," croaked Lewis, his throat dry.

They went down the central path of the cemetery. Halfway to Belle Frisson's strange monument, Uncle Jonathan turned his light to the left. "What in the world is that?" he asked, and he walked between the headstones towards something long, brown, and snaky. Lewis heard a dry rustle as Jonathan picked up whatever it was. Then there was a rattling sound, and in a moment Jonathan was back.

"What is it?" asked Mrs Zimmermann, shining her light towards Jonathan.

"It's a scroll," answered Jonathan. "A long, dry, brown scroll, made of parchment, I think."

"That's the one we saw in the museum!" cried Lewis. "The testament of Belle Frisson I told you about! Oh, my gosh, Rose Rita must have stolen it back again!"

"Don't jump to conclusions," said Mrs Zimmermann. "Here, hold my torch."

Lewis took it and shone it on the parchment as Mrs Zimmermann unrolled it a little at a time. "Hmm," she murmured, and "Oh," and "Aha."

"Come on, Haggy," complained Uncle Jonathan. "This crumply paper means something to you. Tell us what the deal is!"

"It's a spell of unsealing," she said slowly. "Its function is to unlock magically sealed secret places. But it's strangely incomplete. And the parchment seems oddly . . . *stretched*. It's as if it had been used in a tug-of-war by demons. I think all its magic may have been used up."

"Let's go," said Jonathan urgently, taking the

rolled-up scroll from her. "Let's see what else we can find."

They circled the monument. When he turned his torch on the central pillar, Lewis thought it looked different somehow, chipped and rugged. Then he realised that the carvings were no longer there. The stone looked as if someone had taken a hammer and a chisel and pulverised the pillar's surface, erasing all the markings. He moved the circle of his torch lower and saw that a litter of stone chips now covered the top of the cube on which the pillar rested.

Mrs Zimmermann touched his shoulder. "Lewis," she said in a strange voice, "switch off your light. You too, Jonathan."

Lewis did, and the darkness fell like a velvet curtain. Off in the distance an owl cried out, a low, lonesome *Hu-hu-huuuu*! Very faintly came a faraway train whistle, mournful and low. "Look up," said Mrs Zimmermann in little more than a whisper. "Look at that globe on top of the pillar."

Squinting into the darkness, Lewis felt the

hair on his neck and arms bristle. The dark stone sphere at the top of the pillar was—*steaming*. Green, faintly glowing vapours boiled from it, tendrils of mist that thinned and vanished as they evaporated. Jonathan cleared his throat. "Something is going on here," he said. "Something evil. Are those fumes the ones you'd get from the Lamp of Osiris spell?"

"A-plus, Jonathan," replied Mrs Zimmermann. "And you know what that means."

"I don't," said Lewis in a hushed tone.

Mrs Zimmermann turned her torch back on as Jonathan walked around the grave. "It means sacrifice," she said. "Someone has been killed here. Oh, maybe not lately—not this year, or even this century. Still, an unholy rite was performed here. That's the kind of light people used to call a 'corpse candle,' or sometimes a 'will-o'-the-wisp.' It's a product of sudden death—a kind of unfocused haunting."

From the other side of the monument, Jonathan Barnavelt called, "Take a look at this."

They went around. Jonathan was shining his torch at the ground. There, resting on the grass, were a torch, two waxed-paper-wrapped sandwiches and a green-bound book. Jonathan picked it up, and opened it. "*Forty Years Among the Magicians*," he read aloud. He leafed through the book. "It has a chapter on Belle Frisson," he said.

"Rose Rita got that from Mr Hardwick at the museum," Lewis recollected. "So she *has* been back here."

Mrs Zimmermann turned the beam of her torch back towards the tomb. "I'll bet anything she brought the scroll and worked the spell. Or the spell worked itself, more likely. Lewis, is that pillar all bashed up?"

"Yes," said Lewis, "it is. It had marks on it—carvings that didn't really make any sense. They're all gone now."

"A self-activating spell," said Mrs Zimmermann thoughtfully. "Wherever Rose Rita is, she's gone through some magical portal. We've got to find out how to follow."

"How do we do that?" asked Jonathan, sounding frustrated and angry. "You said all the magic is gone from the parchment scroll."

"We do it," said Mrs Zimmermann, "by becoming detectives. Jonathan, Lewis, we can't do anything else here, at least not tonight. I have an idea or two about discovering how to work that spell again—because a magician *can* activate the spell, you know. It doesn't have to work itself. However, I have to figure out exactly how it was worded, and that might take some time. Let's head home. We have until Friday night." *Four days*, thought Lewis. *Only four more days!*

As soon as school was over on Tuesday, Lewis hurried home. Mrs Zimmermann was there, sitting at the dining-room table. She had stacks of paper around her, and she had scribbled all over them. The scroll was there too, looking very fragile and brittle now. Jonathan Barnavelt sat quietly on the other side of the table, deeply engrossed in the book he had retrieved from the cemetery. He looked up and gave Lewis a weak smile. "Hi," he said.

"Have you done it?" asked Lewis.

"Partly," responded Mrs Zimmermann. She looked exhausted. Her wrinkled face was strained and drawn. "From the picture of the tomb in that book, and from the parts of the letters on the scroll, I've got about eighty-five per cent of the spell figured out." She showed Lewis how the edges of the scroll had been meant to line up with the carvings on the tomb. Together, the markings on the tomb and the scroll came together to make up letters, which literally spelled out the incantation. The trouble was that some of the markings on the scroll were just vertical lines. There was no telling if they were meant to be the downwards strokes of T's or I's, or perhaps lower-case l's. Other markings might be the tops of F's or E's, or of B's or R's. Guesswork could fill in a lot of the words, but some were very strange indeed.

Mrs Zimmermann rubbed her eyes. "If only

I knew what the tomb markings were," she said. "That would make life easy!"

"Can't we try what you've got?" asked Lewis. "It might work!"

Jonathan shook his head. "Sorry, Lewis. It has to be the complete spell or nothing. You see, a spell controls and binds the magic. If you tried a spell without all the words, it might not work at all, or the magic might react in uncontrollable ways. You might accidentally turn yourself into a frog, or let demons loose in the world, or produce a live chicken from under your robes."

Lewis groaned.

With a forced laugh Jonathan said, "I'm sorry about that chicken joke. I'm tired, I guess. I'll fix us some dinner, and then we'll go back to studying this sinister scroll."

Mrs Zimmermann pushed a stack of papers away. "I'll fix the dinner," she said. "I'm tired of Fuzzy Face's gourmet ham sandwiches! Tell me what the book says about Belle Frisson while I cook, Jonathan."

Jonathan summarised for them. The information was meagre and not very helpful. "The author of the book thought she was probably just another trickster," Jonathan finished, "although he admitted she did some very startling and baffling effects. No wonder. Clearly, Elizabeth Proctor—or Belle Frisson, as she called herself—was in touch with mysterious powers and forces. There's one odd thing. She seems to have amassed a fortune over the years, but it was all spent on her funeral. Years before her fatal accident she'd arranged for a strange troupe of people to come whenever and wherever she died to prepare her tomb and bury her. That sounds like she was plotting something."

"I agree," said Mrs Zimmermann, rattling pots and pans. "I believe Belle Frisson was determined to come back from the dead."

"I think you've hit it, Florence," declared Jonathan. He turned and stared at the kitchen calendar. "She died on Halloween 1878. I think she's planning to come back this Halloween.

So on Friday at midnight, when the date changes from the thirtieth to the thirty-first—"

He left the rest of the thought unspoken. He didn't need to say any more. The idea was too terrible to put into words.

MADAME FRISSON:
HER TESTAMENT FROM BEYOND
THE GRAVE

CHAPTER FOURTEEN

Rose Rita rose from unconsciousness like a diver slowly swimming to the surface of deep, dark waters. Her first impression was that she had been dreaming. Everything that had happened since the day she had first found the scroll seemed faraway and hazy, like a dimly recalled nightmare. For just a few seconds, Rose Rita felt safe and cosy and warm.

Then she opened her eyes to the repellent green sight, and she knew it had all been real. She found herself sitting on one of the two thrones, and she tried to get up. She could not stir. She could barely even move her head. She looked down at herself, and her eyes grew wide with terror.

Rose Rita's whole body had been wrapped in glistening spider silk. Except for her head she was encased in a cocoon. She might have been a mummy, wrapped in yards and yards of bandages pulled tight around her. Her stomach lurched as she remembered the touch of that huge spider's prickly legs on her shoulders. It had spun its silk around her, the way an ordinary garden spider would spin silk around a trapped insect. Even her hair felt as if it had been plastered to the back of the throne with more silk. Rose Rita had just enough slack to breathe. Her arms had been tied to the arms of the throne, her hands bound to two balls that felt like polished metal. She could not even turn her head.

From the corner of her eye she could glimpse another figure, seated beside her. It was the horrible spider-crawling skeleton. From it came a breathy voice: "There is no need to struggle. You will have no lasting pain, and after that you will not even care. Your mind will continue to work as your body withers away, slowly, slowly, over a hundred years. Its life force will feed me. You will be a part of me in a way. You should be flattered."

"Let me go," said Rose Rita. No longer terrified, no longer paralysed, now she was just plain angry. "You let me go, or you'll be sorry!"

The insinuating voice ignored her. "What will you think of, here in the dark, as I have been for all these years? I believe you will go mad very quickly. Alone in the tomb, with only a spider for company. Yes, I believe you will be quite insane before many weeks have passed."

Rose Rita did not answer. She struggled fiercely to break free, but the clinging spider silk was tough. She could barely wriggle. "Let me go!" she yelled again.

"Foolish child," sneered the voice. "When my body was broken, I reached through the curtain of death to work my will. At my bidding was my tomb fashioned, and at my bidding did my slaves sacrifice one who had been my best friend to Neith, the Weaver of the World. Do you think that I, who would not hesitate to command that, would allow you to escape? No, child, you are my lifeline, my tie to the world. Not for all the treasures would I release you!" The voice chortled, a harrowing, raspy sound. "When the time comes, and it is very close now, my pet will seize you and bend you forwards. It will bite you just once, on the back of the neck, and I am afraid that will be very painful. Then I shall leave you. Behold, already I grow strong."

Rose Rita gritted her teeth to keep from crying out. The skeleton beside her *moved*! With creaky, slow jerks, it raised itself to its feet. It took a wobbling step, and Rose Rita shut her eyes.

The tiny spiders had woven a skin of white spider-web over the skeleton. They were beneath it, for the creature's flesh literally crawled. The empty eye sockets glowed with a red inner light. The mouth had become a straight slit, revealing dry, yellowed teeth. Beneath the linen robe the chest heaved, as if the monstrous thing were breathing.

"You do not think I am lovely?" mocked the voice. "Wait, child. When you have been . . . prepared, when I draw strength and sustenance from you, then this flesh will seem as real as yours. I shall be beautiful! I shall walk the Earth again! This time I shall master the weak mortals around me. After your usefulness has been drained, there will be another, and another. I shall live forever!"

Rose Rita opened her eyes. The skeleton stood before her, swaying, as if it were hardly strong enough to stand. It stepped aside, collapsing back on to the throne with a muffled clatter of bones. "My pet is coming," the voice whispered.

With dread in her heart Rose Rita glared out at the room. Creeping over the round platform was the enormous spider. "No!" screamed Rose Rita.

"The time draws near," said the voice. "The time draws very near."

By Friday, the day before Halloween, Lewis was growing frantic. The police were searching everywhere for Rose Rita, without success. Mr and Mrs Pottinger had offered a reward, but of course that would do no good. Jonathan and Mrs Zimmermann were at the end of their rope. They had tried everything from books on cryptography and code breaking to the most powerful spells that Mrs Zimmermann could think of, but nothing helped.

Lewis stayed home from school that day, too anxious to attend. Late that afternoon the phone rang, and Jonathan answered it. He came back to the kitchen, where Mrs Zimmermann and Lewis waited, with his face set in a grim expression. "That was George Pottinger," he said. "The police have found something after all. A woman named Seidler picked up a girl who said her name was Rowena Potter out west of town, and she dropped her off near the cemetery. The state police searched around and found Rose Rita's bicycle in a cornfield. Now they believe that Rose Rita has run away."

Mrs Zimmermann sighed. "Oh, if only we knew the rest of this blasted spell. I think I have everything except seven words, but they are words of power. Jonathan, if worst comes to worst, we simply have to work the spell. God help us, I don't know what it might do, but we'll have to try."

Lewis said, "Why don't we ask Mr Hardwick if he has pictures?"

Both Jonathan and Mrs Zimmermann looked at him. "Pictures?" asked Uncle Jonathan. "You mean pictures of the monument?"

Mrs Zimmermann asked, "Why do you think he'd take pictures?"

With a shrug, Lewis answered, "I know it's a long shot. Still, Mr and Mrs Hardwick visit the cemetery a lot, and they have friends buried there. And Mr Hardwick does make a point of collecting everything he can about magic— everything from wands and books to posters and Houdini's old milk can."

Jonathan got to his feet. "It's worth a try. Let me call him." He went to the study and made the call, and a minute later he was back. "Let's go!" he hastened them. "Lewis may have saved the day."

Mrs Zimmermann did not even object when Jonathan opened the garage. They drove the few blocks to the National Museum of Magic in Jonathan's boxy old car, and they hurried inside. Mr Hardwick was waiting there for them. He opened the door and ushered them in. "Welcome, welcome," he said, shaking hands with all of them. "Jonathan, it's good to see you again. My, I did admire that trick you did at the Chamber of Commerce meeting last summer—the floating handkerchief. I think I've about figured out how you did it, but it was a great stunt. I—"

With a tight smile Jonathan said, "Thank you very much, Bob, but we'd really like to see— what we talked about on the phone, if it isn't too much trouble."

"Oh, sure," replied Mr Hardwick, leading them to a doorway. "They're in the basement. Has your friend turned up yet, Lewis?"

"No," Lewis said mournfully.

"I'm sorry." Mr Hardwick opened the door and reached inside to flick on a light. "Come on, and watch your step. The stairs are pretty steep. Well, I'm sure Rose Rita will show up. She probably ran away from home. Lots of young people do that, and most of them return again safe and sound." As he talked, Mr Hardwick led them down into a brick-walled cellar. It was lined with dozens of filing cabinets, each drawer labelled. Mr Hardwick waved at them. "This is my collection of letters and manuscripts," he explained. "There are also playbills and advertisements for magic shows. Photographs of famous magicians, many of them autographed. Scrapbooks and handwritten instructions about how to perform tricks. And this one, of course. This cabinet is full of rubbings."

He pulled open a file drawer and rummaged inside, finally producing a thick green folder. "Is that it?" asked Jonathan urgently.

"Yes," replied Mr Hardwick. "The folder is

labelled right here: RUBBING OF THE BELLE FRISSON TOMB." He opened the file and took out a big sheet of thin paper Lewis stared as his uncle took one end of it and unfolded it. The sheet was actually several sheets taped together, and it had been smeared with charcoal.

Lewis realised that it was a tombstone rubbing—Mr Hardwick had placed the paper against the shaft of Belle Frisson's monument and had rubbed a piece of charcoal back and forth over it. The result was a replica in charcoal of all the markings. Mrs Zimmermann was already tracing her finger over the lines of marks. "That's one!" she said.

There were many more folded sheets of paper in the folder, one for each side of the shaft. Mrs Zimmermann found another partial word, then another and another. In five minutes, she had found them all. "Thank you!" she said to a puzzled-looking Mr Hardwick. "Now we have to go!"

Mr Hardwick gave her a curious smile. "Can't

you even tell me why this was so urgent?" he asked.

Jonathan Barnavelt clapped him on the shoulder. "Later, Bob. Right now, all I can say is thank goodness you're such a fanatical collector—and thank you for being so fantastically well organised! Lewis, come on!"

Lewis followed him up the stairs. He realised two things. First, it was terribly late—the sun was ready to set.

Second, Mrs Zimmermann now had the complete spell. They had to go back to the deserted cemetery. They had to use that spell to try to save Rose Rita.

And what would happen? What would they face in that terrifying graveyard? A Death Spider? A sorceress returned from beyond the tomb?

Or something even worse—something so horrible that Lewis could not even imagine it?

CHAPTER FIFTEEN

Jonathan Barnavelt drove like a madman. Lewis hung on as the old car lurched around curves, its tyres screeching. Farmhouses and fields flashed past. The sun was setting as they turned into the long lane that led to the cemetery, and by the time Jonathan had slammed on the brakes and brought his car to a halt, it had vanished.

"We don't have much time," said Mrs Zimmermann, climbing out of the car. "Here, Jonathan. Put this around your neck. Here's yours, Lewis, and here's one for me." From her collection of amulets Mrs Zimmermann had selected three. One was a scarab, an ancient Egyptian symbol of life. Another was a tiny gold cross that had been blessed by a very holy monk in the fifteenth century. The third amulet—the one she gave to Lewis—was a purple gemstone that glowed with a spark of her own magic.

She strode towards the monument carrying a plain black umbrella. It was folded, and its handle was a bronze griffin's talon gripping a crystal sphere. Jonathan and Lewis joined her as she carefully placed the umbrella on the ground. "Hold my hands," she said in a low voice. "Whatever happens, we are in this together."

"All for one," said Lewis in a timid voice. He tried to sound brave, but the attempt was as complete a failure as his magic act had been.

"And one for all," boomed Jonathan Barnavelt. "Florence, do your best. And let any wandering bogies, beasties, and creepy-crawling spiders look out!" He squeezed Lewis's hand, then took Mrs Zimmermann's right hand in his. Lewis held her left hand.

In a clear, high voice Mrs Zimmermann began to pronounce the words of the spell. Some were in English, some in Latin, some in Greek, and some in Coptic, a language spoken in Egypt. Lewis felt the earth beneath his feet shift as the words rang out. He heard a strange groaning, the sound that stone might make if it came to life and tried to stir. And as Mrs Zimmermann pronounced the final syllables of the chant, he saw the sphere on top of Belle Frisson's monument shake. It split into fragments with a great *crack*! and an explosion of dust. Lewis shouted in alarm. The pillar teetered and fell, and the cube of granite slowly pivoted to one side.

It revealed a dark opening leading down into the earth.

Mrs Zimmermann cleared her throat. "So far so good," she said. "Let's go—and watch out for surprises. I'm sure Elizabeth Proctor would have some nasty watchdogs guarding her privacy! Lewis, if we should run into that huge spider, remember it's hardly real at all. It is made up of a pinch of ashes and one drop of living blood. It's just a spectre."

"Th-then it can't hurt us?" asked Lewis.

Mrs Zimmermann's expression was grave. "It can hurt us, all right," she said. "As a spectre, it grows on bad emotions—hatred, fear, and anger. But it must have your belief to exist at all. If you don't believe, you take away its evil power. Remember that . . . Everyone OK? Let's go." She picked up her umbrella, looking ready for action.

Jonathan Barnavelt led the way, his torch sending its strong beam down the tunnel, over the split and decaying tile walls, where green slime had grown. Over the horrible floor of rubbery toadstools. Over the whitened bones of small animals.

Lewis followed him, and Mrs Zimmermann brought up the rear. The stench was appalling, and Lewis felt nauseated. He kept gulping air through his mouth. They followed the twisting tunnel for a long time, and then Jonathan halted. "Here's her watchdog, all right," he whispered. "Florence, see what you think!"

Lewis looked around from behind his uncle. What he saw froze the blood in his veins. The end of the tunnel was completely closed off by a billowing white spider-web, and resting in the exact centre of it was a huge spider. It was not the one they had glimpsed at Rose Rita's house, because that one had been hairy and grey. This one was shiny black, and it had a red hourglass marking on its belly. It was a black widow, the deadliest spider in America.

And it was the size of a dinner plate. Its long legs stirred, and it began to creep down the web.

Mrs Zimmermann stepped forwards and held her umbrella in front of her. Suddenly the umbrella became a dark, long staff, crowned with a blinding sphere of purple light. Mrs Zimmermann changed too—she wore flowing purple robes, with flames in the folds, and she stood tall and terrible. The spider seemed to sense that something was happening. It leaped forwards, its legs stretched wide. Power crackled from Mrs Zimmermann. A bolt of purple energy shot from her hand and struck the hideous creature in mid-air. It tumbled away from them, bursting into flame, and it hit the web. With a *whoosh*! the web caught fire and sizzled away. The spider's body fell to the floor, a sputtering cinder.

Mrs Zimmermann lowered the staff, and it was just an umbrella again. "She knows we're coming now," she said. "Let's not disappoint her!"

They stepped into a large round room. They could not see the far side because of a marble platform in the centre. Slowly they edged around it. Then Mrs Zimmermann stopped with a despairing cry. Lewis stared.

Rose Rita sat on a golden throne. Her body had been wrapped up like a mummy. Her eyes, behind the black-rimmed glasses, were wide with horror. The grey spider, far larger than it had been earlier, crouched above her. Its forelegs rested on her shoulders. Its dripping fangs were only inches from her neck. It clung to the wall, its abdomen pulsing slowly.

A figure stepped around the platform. "Fools," it said in a scornful, breathy voice. Lewis could not believe his eyes. The figure was like the dried corpse of a woman. The flesh was dead white and clung to the bones of the face. The eyes looked hollow, and the mouth was simply a dark slit. It moved as the creature said, "You are too late."

"No," proclaimed Jonathan. "I don't believe we are. Rose Rita, we're here! We've come to take you home!"

"You ignorant man!" exclaimed the walking corpse. "You three will join my guest here—join her for all eternity!"

"Let Rose Rita go," Mrs Zimmermann said, stepping forwards. "You don't want her. Take me instead."

"Why should I do that?" asked the creature.

"Because I am what you always desired to be," replied Mrs Zimmermann. "I am a witch."

Light seemed to flare in the empty eye sockets of the thing that had once been Belle Frisson. "I shall have you *and* the girl," she said. "There is no bargain!"

Lewis saw Rose Rita start to squirm. She twisted, just under the fangs of the spider. Fiercely, she cried out, "You leave Mrs Zimmermann alone! I take back all my bad wishes! I take back that drop of blood! I won't let you hurt my friends!"

The walking corpse whirled, hissing. Mrs Zimmermann said, "So Rose Rita reclaims her drop of blood! Now I can deal with you, my friend!" She raised her umbrella, and from it a spark of intense purple fire leaped out. It struck across the room like a crackling bolt of purple lightning, and it hit the spider above Rose Rita squarely in the back.

Lewis screamed. The creature sprang from the wall, its legs thrashing madly. It scrambled towards them.

Mrs Zimmermann was shouting a spell. Jonathan rushed around the spider and charged to help Rose Rita. The spider reared high over Mrs Zimmermann, who thrust her hand out. Her fingers pierced the spider's skin. Then she jerked her hand away. The tip of one finger was red. "In Rose Rita's name, I reclaim her blood!" she shouted. "You have no power here!"

The mummy of Belle Frisson shrieked from somewhere in the darkness. The spider swayed for an instant, and then its skin cracked into a thousand zigzag lines. The creature collapsed in a dark cloud. In an instant it had vanished.

Jonathan had picked up Rose Rita. The cobwebs that had bound her were vanishing too, crumbling into powder. Jonathan yelled, "Look out, Florence!"

Too late! The mummified Belle Frisson had surged forwards. Bony hands closed around the umbrella. With superhuman strength the shambling creature wrestled it away from Mrs Zimmermann. She wailed and fell to her hands and knees.

Laughing insanely, the undead Belle Frisson raised the umbrella over her head. "A magician's staff breaks when she dies!" the creature screeched. "And sometimes it works the other way! If I smash this globe, you are dead!"

"Wait!" Lewis cried, stepping forwards. His knees were knocking. He felt as if he were about to faint. But he knew he had to keep Belle Frisson from shattering the umbrella. He held up his empty hands. "Wait!" he said again. "I have a gift for you!"

"What?" The red eye sockets seemed to bore into him. "What would you have?"

"A talisman!" Lewis shouted, his voice breaking. "See, it's here! It's in my hand!"

"There is nothing in your hand!"

"That's because it's invisible!" Lewis screamed. "I am the Mystifying Mysto! Now you don't see it"—he flicked his hand, doing a movement he had practised over and over for the magic show—"and now you do! Take that!" The powerful amulet swung out from his jacket. He grabbed it, lunged forwards, and thrust it against the shambling creature's face!

The purple star flared to brilliant life. The

living corpse howled as the crystal burned into her, creating a sizzling hole right between her eye sockets. She dropped the umbrella, which Lewis barely managed to catch.

"Get back!" yelled Mrs Zimmermann, pulling Lewis away.

The creature staggered. Purple beams of light shone from her eyes, from her gaping mouth. Her skin billowed, crisped, burned away. Then she collapsed to a pile of bones; and in a silent, purple explosion, she flew into whirling dust.

The ground began to shake. Mrs Zimmermann took her umbrella from Lewis, and the globe gave off its strong purple glow. "Rose Rita, are you all right?"

"I am now!" said Rose Rita.

"Let's get out of here," bellowed Uncle Jonathan. "This place is caving in!"

They raced for the tunnel. Lewis did not look back. From behind him came awful sounds of collapse and ruin, and he did not wish to see what was producing them.

CHAPTER SIXTEEN

"Is she really gone?" asked Rose Rita. Two weeks had passed since the underground struggle with the animated corpse of Belle Frisson, and she was still having nightmares.

"Yes!" replied Mrs Zimmermann decisively. "We snapped her thread, you might say. She had connected her spirit to the land of the living with a magic spell, like a spider's web. When Lewis did his magic trick, he burned right through that magical web. Her spirit was banished to the domains of the dead, and that's why everything fell apart."

"Don't tell anyone around here that, though," said Jonathan Barnavelt with a laugh. "They all think it was a mighty unusual earthquake that toppled her monument!"

"We got out just in time," said Lewis.

It was an unseasonably warm Saturday in November. The four friends were sitting in the back garden of 100 High Street, enjoying the balmy warm day. Mrs Zimmermann had baked a big plate of delicious double-fudge walnut brownies, and they were all munching happily and drinking tall glasses of milk. Rose Rita's sudden return had astonished everyone in New Zebedee, but she had risen to the occasion. She concocted a story of tumbling off her bike and getting amnesia. For several days, she told everyone, she had wandered around not knowing who she was. She said she had slept in barns.

Jonathan told the police that he, Mrs Zimmermann, and Lewis had found Rose Rita when they had driven over the route that Mrs Seidler had talked about. Rose Rita, who had been without food and water for several days, had to spend that Friday night in the hospital, but she made a rapid recovery. Even the tiny moon-shaped mark where she had cut her finger faded and vanished. Now everything at her house was more or less back to normal, except that Mrs Pottinger would not allow Rose Rita to ride her bike for the rest of the autumn and winter. Rose Rita said that was a small price to pay.

"Did you replace the scroll?" Mrs Zimmermann asked.

"When I took the book back to Mr Hardwick, I slipped the scroll into its box," Rose Rita admitted. "Do you really think it's safe now?"

"Yes. All its magic power is gone," Mrs Zimmermann said. "Without that, the scroll is just a curiosity. And now that the tomb has been destroyed in the cave-in, it can't cause any more mischief."

Jonathan looked at Lewis. "You're very quiet," he said. "What are you thinking?"

Lewis grinned. "I'm thinking that I did pretty good for an amateur magician," he said. "I fooled Belle Frisson into letting me get close, and then I used the chicken trick to hit her with that amulet."

"That was fast thinking," Rose Rita said. "How did you know it would work?"

Lewis shrugged. "I didn't know—not really," he confessed. "Only it seemed to me that Mrs Zimmermann's magic is good, and that it would destroy evil. So I took a chance. I didn't know what else to do."

"Your instincts were right on the money," said Mrs Zimmermann. "I'm glad you didn't let her smash my umbrella. Ugh! It might not have killed me, but such a blow wouldn't have left me the same."

Rose Rita kept glancing around the yard nervously. Jonathan tilted his head and asked, "What's wrong, Rose Rita?"

She scowled. "I don't know. I keep having the creepy feeling that I'm being watched, but I guess that's impossible. Old Belle Frisson is long gone, and I hope her spiders have gone with her!"

"I'm sure they have," said Mrs Zimmermann. She looked thoughtful. "Hmm. Now that you mention it, I think I have a sense of being watched too. Weird Beard, do you want to have a stab at finding out why?"

Grinning, Jonathan Barnavelt made a couple of magic passes. In the air in front of him a golden arrow appeared, floating with no support. It looked like an old-fashioned weather-vane. It spun around and around, and it wound up pointing towards the corner of the house. Jonathan got up and winked as the arrow disappeared. He tiptoed over to the house. Then he pounced, and Lewis heard a squeak.

Jonathan reappeared, chuckling. "Come along," he said. Chad Britton came around the corner, wearing his trench coat and looking embarrassed. "Cheer up," said Jonathan to the others. "It's only our neighbourhood detective!"

"Chad, were you spying on us?" asked Lewis.

"No, not really," Chad said. "I just—well, I—I thought—"

Mrs Zimmermann reached for the tray of

brownies. "You thought you detected the smell of fudge," she said kindly.

"Yeah!" said Chad, beaming.

"Have one," Mrs Zimmermann told him. "And next time just come up and ask."

Chad bit into a brownie and rolled his eyes. "This is great," he said. "Thanks, Mrs Zimmermann!"

"You're welcome," replied Mrs Zimmermann.

Lewis reached for a brownie too. "Well," he said, "maybe Chad and I are both on the right track. He detected these brownies, so he'd be a good detective. And I'm a great magician. Watch me make this brownie disappear!"

Chad laughed, and Rose Rita and the others joined in. The pleasant sound topped off a wonderful day.

The End

John Bellairs (1938–1991) was an award-winning American author of many gothic mystery novels for children and young adults, including *The House With a Clock in Its Walls*, which received both the New York Times Outstanding Book of the Year Award and the American Library Association Children's Books of International Interest Award, *The Lamp from the Warlock's Tomb*, which won the Edgar Award and *The Spectre from the Magician's Museum*, which won the New York Public Library 'Best Books for Teen Age' Award.

Brad Strickland has written more than eighty-five published books, including entries in the Lewis Barnavelt and Johnny Dixon series, following the death of the original series creator, John Bellairs. He is a Professor Emeritus of English and lives in Georgia with his wife, Barbara.

Have you read the previous book?

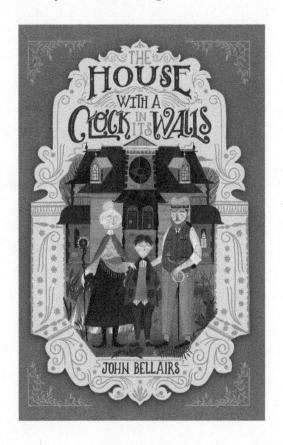

Have you read the previous book?

Piccadilly
PRESS

Have you read the previous book?

Piccadilly
PRESS

Have you read the previous book?

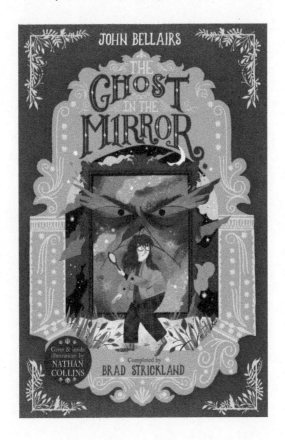

Piccadilly
PRESS

Have you read the previous book?

Piccadilly
PRESS

Have you read the previous book?

Piccadilly
PRESS

Look out for more magic from
Lewis and Rose Rita

THE BEAST UNDER THE WIZARD'S BRIDGE

When Lewis and Rose Rita explore old Wilder Creek Bridge and the deserted farm nearby, they discover shocking secrets: the destruction of the bridge threatens to release a horrifying monster. Can Lewis, Rose Rita, Uncle Jonathan and Mrs Zimmermann vanquish this ferocious creature?

Coming in 2020

Thank you for choosing a Piccadilly Press book.

If you would like to know more about our authors, our books or if you'd just like to know what we're up to, you can find us online.

www.piccadillypress.co.uk

And you can also find us on:

We hope to see you soon!